W9-ABP-144

Cedar Crest College
Library
Allentown, Pennsylvania

Presented by

Cedar Crest College

Alumnae

L-D

SECRET OF THE ANDES

SECRET
OF THE
ANDES

BY ANN NOLAN CLARK
WITH DRAWINGS BY JEAN CHARLOT

1952
THE VIKING PRESS · NEW YORK

Copyright 1952 by Ann Nolan Clark
First published by The Viking Press in March 1952
Published on the same day in the Dominion of Canada
by The Macmillan Company of Canada Limited
Second printing February 1953
Third printing July 1953
Fourth printing March 1954
Fifth printing January 1957
Sixth printing September 1959
Seventh printing July 1961

Title page and end-papers lithographed in the United States of America
by Reehl Litho Company
Text printed in the United States of America
by the Vail-Ballou Press, Inc.

J
F
C 592s

CONTENTS

SECRET OF THE ANDES

1. HIDDEN VALLEY

"What are you doing, Cusi?" An old Indian stood looking down at a boy who lay on an overhanging rock, gazing into the valley below. The old Indian's slow, deep voice broke the stillness of the mountain world.

At the sound the young boy leaped to his feet. His dark face was shining with happiness. His black eyes danced with excitement. "Oh, Chuto," he answered, "Chuto, I see them again." At Chuto's questioning look he said, "Sometime every day I come here to watch them. Look, Old One, if you lie flat on this rock and lean far forward you can see them too."

The old Indian bent low over the rock and looked down to

the deep, deep valley so far below. "Ah," he said and repeated it again. "Ah!"

In the valley a family of Indians had cleared the land for a small field and a smaller hut. There were five of them, a man, a woman, and three children. From where the boy crouched on the rock ledge at the head of the zigzag trail, the Indians looked so small they seemed almost antlike. Chuto could see them distinctly.

"Yes," Cusi whispered. "Yes, you see them. People!" The young voice broke in wonder. The whispered echo, "People," like a smoke ring from a campfire, circled upward, getting larger, getting fainter, until it misted in the cold, blue air.

"I have not seen people before, not that I remember. Isn't it wonderful that I can come here and see them every day, Chuto? Isn't it wonderful!"

The old man got up stiffly from his place on the rock. It was true. The boy had seen no people in the eight years he had lived here. He had been too young to remember what had gone before. Chuto looked around at the world that so tightly enclosed them.

They lived in a hidden valley high up on the rock slope of a mountain. Mountain peak upon mountain peak, sheer and hard and glistening in frozen mantles of ice and snow, encircled them. There were but two openings into their hidden world. One, where they stood now, was the head of the llama trail. It was a narrow, rocky path that zigzagged steeply down the slope. At its foot, more than a mile below them, lay the little valley where the people were.

At the far end of Hidden Valley was the second opening. From where he stood Cusi could not see this second opening. He only knew it was there.

Morning clouds softened the tips of the mountain peaks. Here and there the cloud mists parted. Then patches of blue sky could be seen, and snow peaks, sharp and pointed and sparkling against the blue.

Hundreds of llamas were munching the moss-green ychu grass that covered the floor of the highland valley. They made spots of golden yellow against the soft green of the ychu and the glaring white of the glacier snow fields.

The old man brought his look back to the boy beside him. "You miss people, my Cusi?" The old man's words scarcely rippled the pool of silence they were spoken so gently and so low.

"I cannot tell you, sir, since I know no people," the boy answered and would have said more, but Chuto spoke again. "It's time," he said and then repeated as was his habit. "Yes, it is now time, I think."

Through the stillness of the morning came faintly the wailing song of Panpipes. Cusi looked his surprise. No one lived in this hidden valley but himself and the Old One who loved him as a son.

Chuto smiled at the boy's amazement. "I came to tell you," he said. "A wandering minstrel has found us in our mountain world."

Cusi was delighted. "You have told me so many times that some day he would come. Where is he? Will he say his poems? Will he sing his songs? Will he make music on the Pipes of Pan?"

In his excitement Cusi would have gone running across the ychu grass to greet the visitor. Chuto stopped him.

"Wait," he said. "Do not run from me. I came to tell you to come and we would let the minstrel sing the hours away for us. Now I have another plan. This one, perhaps, is better."

Cusi waited. He wondered what could be better than seeing a wandering minstrel. "Yes," the Old One said. "This is better, I think. You and I, Cusi, will go on a journey. We will journey down the mountain trail to the Salt Pits which lie two valleys beyond."

"Journey?" Cusi could not believe it. "Salt Pits?" he asked. "But our llamas! Who would tend our flock? How can we go and let our llamas stay the many nights it would take us with no herd boy to shepherd them?"

"The minstrel," Chuto answered. "The minstrel will tend them for us. He will be glad to earn his fire and his food until we return. Come. We will tell him."

The old man walked across the mountain meadow of moss-green ychu grass. Cusi followed him. The boy's thoughts were whirling like the foaming rapids on the far side of the valley. To have seen people! To have a wandering minstrel visit them! To go beyond the valley on a journey! These things were happening to him, Cusi, herd boy of the llamas! It was too much! Cusi's thoughts whirled, but his feet followed the footsteps of Chuto as silently, quickly they went across the ychu grass.

The music of the Panpipes was sweeter now. The llamas stopped their grazing and turned to listen. The red woolen tassels in their pointed ears bobbed gaily as they turned their heads. Their eyes were deep, dark pools, beautiful and sad. This music belonged to them. It was their music. It was Inca music as old as the rocks of the canyon walls, as mysterious as the mountains.

Cusi saw the minstrel. He was Indian, with sandals and poncho and gay knitted cap with a tasseled end and bright earflaps. He was an Indian, with shin-length cotton trousers and a woven coca bag. He was Indian as Cusi was Indian, as Chuto was Indian. But he was something more. He bore the fierce look of Inca kings of days that were gone. He bore the proud look of the giant condor circling a cliff nest on a mountain crest. He had the grace of the puma waiting to spring upon its prey. The minstrel was wild and free as sound can be wild and free. Holding the Panpipes lightly, he let his breath dance along the tips of the hollow reeds. The music he coaxed into being stole through the morning air and was answered by the silvery tinkle of the lead llama's bell.

As the man and the boy came near him, the minstrel rose from his seat on the ground. He stopped his music-making and looked at Cusi. "Oho!" he said. "Golden earplugs in the young boy's ears! It is true, then, what they say."

"Who says, and what is said?" Chuto asked. His usually gentle voice was harsh and stern.

The boy looked from one man to the other. What were they talking about? His earplugs, surely. But why? He had always worn them. They were part of him. Did all boys wear them? What made them different?

Chuto was speaking, not in anger now but with his usual softness. "Our Brother comes at a good time. It is well. He will stay here to shepherd our flock while we go to the Salt Pits." Quickly, as if to stop refusal, he added, "Our Brother shows wisdom, perhaps, when he recognizes a symbol of the royal blood. It is time we saw the valley beyond us. Today Cusi saw people in the valley below us. In a week's time he will have seen many. Curiosity can leap the highest wall; an open gate is better. Does not the Singer of Songs agree with me?"

The minstrel's smile lighted up his dark face like sunlight glancing against an eagle's wing. "The stranger remains not strange when words that he already knows are spoken. When do you leave?"

Cusi sat hard upon the ground. This was too much to take without some gesture of acceptance. Chuto and the minstrel looked at him and laughed together.

They understand me when I do not say a word, and I cannot understand them, although their words are many, Cusi thought in bewilderment and envy.

The two men were walking toward the llama corral and the shelter that stood at one end. The shelter was small and rudely built, but it was the only home that Cusi had. He did not think of it as a home. Home was the mountain peaks, the snow fields, the meadow covered with ychu grass. The hut was only a place for storage. Food was kept there, and cooking gourds and clay pots. Yarn Cusi spun was kept there, and the olla for chicha, the sour-sweet drink made of new corn, and the net bag of coca leaves.

Cusi looked at the llamas, grazing again now that the music had stilled. They were the heart of his home. At night he slept among them. Their silky fleece kept him warm and dry. Their nearness kept him unafraid. By day they gave him company. When they were pleased, they hummed for him. When they were resting, they chewed their cuds and looked at him. They understood his words and his moods. They obeyed his commands. They were his companions. Cusi was not certain that he wanted to leave them even for a day. He was not certain he wanted to leave his mountain world for a journey two valleys beyond.

He sat thinking.

Suncca, the thin gray shepherd dog, came to sit beside him. Suncca whined in his young master's ear. He did not like the stranger or his strange music. He was afraid. But Suncca was afraid of everything. His work was not to guard the llamas. His work was to bark and make noise. He was good at that. Cusi put his hand on Suncca's head to comfort him.

Misti, the young black llama that was Cusi's own, came close. His big dark eyes were full of questions. The lead llama's bell went tinkle, tinkle, tinkle. Each in his own way was asking the important question, "Are you going, Cusi?"

"Yes," Cusi answered them. "I am going, but I will be back soon."

Slowly the boy got to his feet and began walking toward the hut where the men had gone.

The sun broke through the clouds, and morning mist melted beneath its shining glory. Rainbow balls of light danced across the snow fields.

Suddenly Cusi felt happy. It would be fun to go on a journey. It would be fun to see what lay beyond the mountains of Hidden Valley. He began to run.

2. SUNRISE CALL

Cusi wakened to the sound of llama-humming. Such a beautiful sound, he thought, even more beautiful than the music the minstrel blew on his Pipes of Pan. Thinking of the minstrel's music made Cusi remember last night. He had sat in the shelter of the hut with Chuto and listened to the minstrel's songs. Last night the minstrel had sung about the stars. He had sung about the Pleiades and how they guarded the new seeds sleeping in the deep earth. He had sung about Venus, page boy to the Sun. He had sung about the Milky Way that was a great river flowing across the heavens. It was here, the minstrel sang, that the great god of the weather dipped his gourd for the water to make it rain. But the best song of all was the one to the group of sister stars called the *orqo-cil-ya*. Cusi remembered the words. Softly he sang them to the llamas' humming.

> "Orqo-cil-ya, Sister Stars,
>   Orqo-cil-ya in the night sky,
>   You are the keepers,
>   the keepers, the keepers,
>   You are the keepers of the llama herd.
>
> "Orqo-cil-ya, Sister Stars,
>   Orqo-cil-ya in the night sky,
>   Guard you the llamas,
>   the llamas, the llamas,
>   Guard you the llamas of my herd."

The llamas stopped humming. Chuto was coming among them. He was greeting them in the Indian way. He was telling them that new day was with them, that they must be up to graze the ychu grass. He came to where Cusi lay snug and warm with his black head cradled in Misti's long black hair.

"This is a new day for you, too, Cusi," Chuto said to the boy. "Today you will come with me to greet the sun." Cusi leaped to his feet, startling Misti with his quick jump. He had wanted many times to go with Chuto into the gray dawn to greet the sunrise. Chuto always before had refused him. He had said, "Not this day. The time has not come." But today it had come. Cusi lost no time in following the old Indian through the flock of resting llamas, across the meadow of ychu grass to the far end of the valley.

The morning was cold with the coldness of before dawn. It was gray with the grayness of before dawn. It felt unfriendly because the world had not yet wakened to make it happy with living things.

Chuto was a dark shadow moving in the gray shadows. Cusi followed him swiftly lest he become lost in the earth clouds that billowed around them.

When they reached the far side of the meadow Chuto turned abruptly into a path between two stunted, twisted trees. Cusi had not been here before because he had not thought that the twisted trees were sentinels to a secret trail. At once the path led downward, steeply downward. It turned and curved and circled among the giant boulders of a canyon wall. Cusi was panting now, partly from excitement and a little from fear of the dark shadows and misted forms and the unsure footing of the unfamiliar secret trail. Suddenly his feet felt firm rock beneath them. He knew he was standing on cold rock steps and then that slowly, carefully, gropingly he was climbing down, climbing down, climbing down.

Suddenly he had reached the bottom. The trail now led through a narrow, deep-walled canyon. A few more steps and they came to the end of the trail. It was brighter now. Cusi looked around, stunned with delight. He and Chuto were standing on a flat tablelike rock of pure white marble. Around them was a circle of tiny trees, gnarled and old and growing huddled together, guarding their secret. Beneath the marble rock lay, quiet and still and dark and deep, a pool of night-black water. There was no sound. There was no movement. No wind blew through the twisted, tangled branches of a tree. No bird chirped its morning prayer. No twig broke beneath the fleet foot of a running fox. No wavelet rippled in the somber pool. Chuto turned to face the eastern sky that arched above the dwarfed tree tops. He waited. Cusi waited. The whole world waited.

Slowly the gray sky turned silvery blue, then golden yellow, then flaming red. The sun, a giant ball of fire, rose in majesty. Chuto raised his arms and chanted his sunrise call as Indian men have chanted since the world was made and the Inca was born. His words rose skyward, word upon word upon word. The world stayed still to listen.

Chuto chanted:

"O Sun! Great Father of the Inca
  who have gone before us.
Great Father of the children of the Inca
  who remain in this thy world.
Forget us not though we are few in number.
Forget us not though our ancient greatness
      is now but a shadow
      in the memory of man.

Forget us not though our ancient pride
is as the dust of the earth
blown before the willful wind.

"O Sun! Great Father of the Inca!
Shine in thy glory upon us in safety.
Shine in thy glory upon us in peace.
Shine in thy glory upon us in wisdom.
Keep our minds clear in thy light.
Keep our hearts young in thy warmth.
Keep our feet straight in thy path,
for we are thy children,
O Sun! O Sun!
Great Father of the Inca."

Chuto finished his chanting. The sun had risen. The old man looked at Cusi. He said, surprisingly enough in his low, sweet everyday voice, "This is where I found you, Cusi, over there in that half-moon of trees. You were so little, all big black eyes and short stiff hair standing up like a cap of spiny black feathers."

Cusi looked at the spot where Chuto pointed. He would have liked to ask questions. He would have liked to talk about the funny baby sitting in the half-moon tree cluster. Who had put him there? Where had he come from? Suddenly he remembered the Indians he had seen in the valley below. They were a family. Chuto had called them a family when he spoke about them to the minstrel. Long ago had Cusi come from such a family? Had there been a man person and a woman person in his family? Had there been other children? Sharply Cusi was brought back to the present by Chuto's voice. He was saying, "Come, Cusi. We go back the way we came. There is but one trail here."

3. LLAMA-HUMMING

The way back seemed shorter now that daylight had come to light the way. It was not long before Chuto and Cusi were walking across the ychu grass toward the thin curl of the smoke of the breakfast fire.

Breakfast and the minstrel and Misti and Suncca were waiting for them. Work was waiting also. While they ate boiled pigweed seeds and tostado made of parched corn, they talked of the coming journey. The minstrel had been to the Salt Pits. He had been to Cuzco, the Holy City. He had been to Lima, the City of Kings. He had been everywhere. It would be great, Cusi thought, to be a minstrel and wander over the land from the place where the sun rose in the morning to the place where it set at evening time. That is, it would be great if one had no llama herd to keep him home.

After breakfast the men and the boy went to the llama corral. It was made of high stone walls. The walls were a part of a ruined temple of the days of old when the Incas ruled Peru, before the Spaniards came. In the corral the mother llamas were kept with their babies that were too young to join the flock grazing in the highland meadow. Only a few months ago Misti, the black one, had lived here with Yellow-Ears, his mother. When Cusi entered the corral, Yellow-Ears came to speak with him. Cusi turned to the minstrel to tell him to be careful here. Yellow-Ears would not like him, Cusi thought, and Yellow-Ears had a way of showing her displeasure. She spat. Cusi started to say, "Keep a distance, Señor. This Yellow-Ears will spit on you." He did not say it. He had no need to say it. Yellow-Ears and the minstrel were friends. They were looking at each other with the look that means "I like you." Cusi was surprised. That minstrel man certainly was wonderful. He must be, if even the llamas in the corral accepted him.

Chuto was busy with the baby llamas. He really did not want to leave them even for the short time the trip to the Salt Pits would take. He was happy here in Hidden Valley and never wanted to go away. Twice a year he went down into the valley beneath them. The first trip was to get the food supplies that were left for him there. The second was on a mysterious errand that he never talked about. These trips took only a day. Since Cusi had come to live with him, Chuto had never been away from his flock for overnight. But this time he must go. Uninvited, the outside world had come to beckon Cusi to go beyond the mountain. Chuto must take him. It had to be done.

Now the old man went among the baby llamas, looking at them and speaking with them. They were a sacred trust. Nothing must happen to them.

Cusi was left to entertain the visitor. "Our mother llamas never carry loads," he told the minstrel importantly.

"I know," the man answered. "You keep them for shearing."

"And to have their babies," Cusi added.

The minstrel nodded. "That Misti fellow of yours is a good one," he said. "Did you know that in the days of the Inca Kings a black llama like yours was always the first to be sacrificed to the Sun?"

Cusi did not know this. He looked worriedly at the corral gate to see if Misti was waiting for him there.

The minstrel went on talking. It seemed that he knew as much about llamas as he did about songs. He knew how to use the llama slingshot. He knew how to turn the llamas' heads inward in a circle before one began to put the loads on their backs. He knew why father llamas were never sheared—so that the long hair on their backs would make matted pads for their loads.

"Did a llama ever sit down and refuse to move for you?" Cusi asked him.

The minstrel said, "No, I myself have never owned a llama. But I have seen them sit down when they were displeased about something." Both he and Cusi laughed at this. There is nothing funnier than to see a string of llamas sitting down on the trail and refusing to move. "Just because one of them has been overloaded," Cusi said.

Chuto called to them. The old Indian was satisfied that all was well with each and every member of his flock. He was ready to return to the hut and finish weaving the mat he had been working on. He was making it of tortoru reeds and twisted grass. It would be good to sleep on when he traveled. Cusi also had work to do. They needed new rope to tie their bundles. Yesterday the boy had gathered armfuls of long grass and had put them to soak in water overnight. Now he pounded the water-soaked grass with a rounded wooden club. When he had mashed it into a pulp, he rolled it into long strands between his hands. Next he braided the strands into even, strong rope lengths.

While he and Chuto worked, the minstrel sang to them. This morning his songs were about the Inca Kings of long ago, when Peru belonged to them and not to the Spaniards who conquered them.

The minstrel played softly at first on his Panpipes, and the grazing llamas stopped to listen. Then, as the music continued, they folded their feet beneath them and rested. They began humming. No music is more beautiful than llama-humming. It sounds like wind over the water. It sounds like water rippling over moss-covered stones. It is wind-and-water music. It made a moving background for the sweet crying of the minstrel's pipes. Cusi stopped braiding the grass strands to listen. Chuto stopped twisting tortoru reeds and long grass to listen. Suncca crouched by his young master and forgot to whine and forgot to be afraid in beauty of the music. The minstrel began to sing, softly at first, then louder and louder to the music of the Panpipes and the llama-humming.

He sang:

"Long ago they made it,
   the world.
It was young.
The people in it,
   the world,
They were new.

"Then the Sun Father
   in kindness
   sent Topa,
   grandfather of the Inca,
   sent Coya,
   queen mother of the Inca,
   to teach them,
   the people.

"Sun Father sent them,
   Topa and Coya,
   saying,

'Take you this golden staff
and walk with it
across the new-made world,
walk with it
until by its own desire
it sinks itself
into the heart of the earth.
There then is your new home.'

"They did as they were told,
Topa and Coya,
and the staff sank itself
in the soft earth
of the place that is known
as Peru,
Four Quarters of the World,
to become home of the Inca."

The minstrel finished his song. The music stopped. Only the
llamas kept on humming.
The echo:

"In—ca
Home—of—the—Inca
Home—of—the—Inca
In—ca
In——ca"

kept bounding from mountain peak to mountain peak.
The song was finished.
The llamas kept humming.

4. SINGER OF SONGS

Chuto put his mat into water; then he weighted it down with stones. Tomorrow it would be ready for taking. He came over to Cusi and bent down to look at the new rope. He measured its length. It was long enough. He ran his thumb and forefinger over it. It was even and rounded. He tested it for strength. It was all right. It was a good rope. He pointed with his lips in the Indian manner. Cusi knew what he meant. There was new work to do, and this task he did not like.

He stood up. He stretched and yawned. He patted Misti. He threw a stone for the dog Suncca to fetch back to him. He looked at Chuto. The old Indian was sorting woven net bags and squares of cloth to take to the Salt Pits. Cusi looked at the minstrel. He was gazing across the snow field. His face was quiet and at peace. He was doing his work. He was singing for fire and for food. It was enough. He was happy.

Cusi wondered what the new Indian family were doing today in their new home in the valley below. He was surprised when Chuto turned to him and spoke quietly. "Come, we will look again at our new neighbors. I, too, need to know how they spend their days." Chuto walked toward the big rock at the head of the llama trail, and Cusi walked beside him. The other work could wait. This was important.

Chuto was first to squat on the overhanging rock ledge, but quickly he made a place for Cusi beside him. The old man and the young boy silently peered down at the scene below them. The family were resting in the shade of their new hut. Smoke from a small fire curled upward in a dark ribbon of blue. The mother sat nearest the fire. She held the smallest child in her arms. The father and the two other children sat facing her. It made a happy picture. Cusi's breath caught sharply. How wonderful it would be to have children to play with and a mother to talk with you. He turned his head away and was glad when Chuto told him, "We have seen enough for today."

Cusi followed the old man slowly as they made their way back to their hut. Just before they reached it, Chuto turned to the boy and said, "They are the ones. Yes, they are the ones to get this year's giving, I think." Cusi did not understand. He stood looking at Chuto, wanting him to explain. Chuto hesitated, walked a few steps, stopped and spoke again. "Llamas," he said. "It is so willed."

This was something to think about. The Old One must mean that every year he gave llamas away. Cusi thought back, remembering the mysterious day-trips Chuto made every once in a long, long time. Yes. Now he remembered clearly that on these trips Chuto would take llamas with him, but he did not bring them back again. He must give them to someone. But why? And who willed that he should do so?

Cusi was glad to begin his new task, although usually he did not like to do it. But today it seemed easier than thinking. Some thoughts are hard to think about.

The boy went into the hut for the sack of frozen potatoes. He dragged the sack out into the morning sunshine. He put handfuls of the small, hard, rocklike potatoes on a flat stone mortar. Then, rocking a rounded hand stone back and forth on the mortar, he ground the frozen potatoes. This would make chuno, their favorite boiled supper dish that they ate every day and every day and every day.

Chuto began making sandals. Both he and Cusi would need them on their way across the mountains. The sandals were easy to make. They were one-piece sandals made of llama hide and tied at the top with leather thongs.

For a while it was very quiet in the mountain meadow. The llamas were grazing. Suncca was sleeping in the sun. Only the grinding sound could be heard as Cusi rocked the pestle back and forth and back and forth.

Then the minstrel began to chant. This time he used no music. His voice was low and sing-song, barely cutting through the quiet. He told of the building of Cuzco, the Holy City of the Inca Kings and their hundred thousand subjects. As he chanted, the city seemed to take shape and grow and become real in the thin misted air of the morning.

Cusi could see it. He could see a city built of walls, of walls of gray stone. Beautiful stones, so perfectly fitted that no mortar was needed to hold them together. Gigantic stones, some weighing as much as twenty tons. Enduring stone, outlasting the Incas, outlasting the conquerors from Spain, outlasting earthquake and flood, outlasting centuries. With the minstrel's words Cusi could see ten thousand men, building for fifty years their majestic palaces of stone. They had no wheels. They had no machinery. They had no tools of building. They had only the power of the Inca and the faith of builders.

The minstrel chanted on and on and on. The hours slipped into the blue haze drifting over the glacier snow fields.

The minstrel told of the Temple to the Sun built at Cuzco and still standing there, crowned with the pride and the years of the ages.

Cusi, the Indian boy, bending over the grinding stone, making chuno of the small bitter potato that fed him, was not here in Hidden Valley. Cusi, the shepherd boy, wiping the sweat from his face with a thin brown arm, was not a boy of the highland meadows. He was not kneeling on ychu grass before a grass-thatched hut. He was a royal child in the Temple to the Sun in Cuzco, Holy City of the Ancients. The magic of the minstrel's words had changed his world. Dressed in cloth of gold, a fringed turban on his head and golden sandals on his feet, he was in the great Sun Temple with its walls of sheeted gold sprinkled with rubies and emeralds. He was walking in the Temple garden where every delicate flower leaf and flower petal had been carved by a master hand from lumps of solid gold. He was watching the Sun Maidens playing papa-aw-ki with their hoop of gold and their golden ball.

The minstrel's voice droned on like the waters of a waterfall splashing against the lichen-covered stones:

> "Maidens of Beauty,
> Maidens of Piety,
> Maidens of Wisdom,
> Maidens of Kindness,
> Come, ye are chosen
> Handmaidens of the Sun.

> "Live in the House of Beauty,
> Live in the House of Precious Metals,
> Live in the House of Gleaming Jewels,
> Live in the House of Gentle Goodness.
> Come, ye are chosen
> Handmaidens of the Sun."

The chuno was made. Every potato in the sack had been ground into a coarse meal. Cusi sat back on his heels and looked at the minstrel. The Indian had finished his chanting and was now solemnly chewing coca leaves. Cusi looked at the llamas in the ychu grass. They had finished their day's grazing and were now solemnly chewing their cuds. Cusi looked around for Chuto. The old Indian was kindling the supper fire. He was holding a small golden disk to catch the last of the sun's rays to light the crumpled dry llama dung. Soon he had a small blaze started. Cusi brought him an armload of dry dung to feed the flame. Then he brought a clay pot filled with chuno. He knew what they would have for supper. It was always the same, parched corn and boiled chuno and afterward a handful of coca leaves and a lump of lime to chew to make the cold night warmer. Cusi did not feel sorry because his food was always the same—frozen potatoes and corn, a gruel made of pigweed seed, and sometimes a stew of dried bits of meat. It was all he had. He was always a little hungry, always a little cold, always a little lonely. He knew no other way of living.

But tonight was special. The minstrel had brought a treat. He had brought a small gourd of chicha, the sweet-sour corn drink of the Andes. The minstrel called it liquid song. It made the evening meal a fiesta.

Cusi was tired. His hands were cut from pounding and pulling and braiding the wet grass strands. His back ached from bending over the grinding stone. But he was happy. Supper had tasted good. The chicha and the coca had made the cold night almost warm.

They sat in comfortable, contented silence, watching the wind blow the night clouds against the snow peaks. "We will leave directly after sunrise in the morning," Chuto said. Cusi was surprised. For the moment he had forgotten the excitement of the coming journey. "I will sing you to sleep," the minstrel promised and at once began his night song, to the wailing of his Panpipes.

"In the days of the Ancients,
  of the Ancients,
  of the Ancients,
  when the last Inca was King,
  ruling his land
  with power,
  with glory,
  with majesty
  since the beginning.

"To the Land of the Inca
  there came men
  of another land,
  of another race,
  of another color,
  of another creed.
They came to conquer the Inca.
They came to subdue the people.
They came to rob their temples.
They came to destroy their gods.

"Then the subjects of the Inca
  sent gold to appease the enemy,
  sent silver to soften the enemy,
  sent emeralds to ransom their king,
  sent rubies to set him free.
On the backs of ten thousand llamas
  they loaded the wealth of the Andes,
  they loaded the metals of the Andes,

they loaded the jewels of the Andes
as ransom for their king,
the Inca.
"But the Spaniards killed the Inca.
They killed the King of the Ancients,
and the ten thousand llamas
and the wealth they carried
disappeared from the earth
forever and forever and forever."

Cusi leaped to his feet. "No, no, no. The ten thousand llamas did not disappear forever. They are here, being taken care of."

Chuto was also standing, "Who told you that?" His voice frightened Cusi.

"I don't know," the boy stammered. "It's something that I've always known, or maybe it's something I dreamed. I don't know, Old One. Should I know?"

The old Indian drew the boy to him. "There are many things we do not know. The time is not now to know," he said vaguely.

The minstrel was smiling at them. His face in the light of the night fire seemed as ageless, as peaceful, as unmoving as the mountain peaks against the night sky.

Chuto looked at him and spoke softly. "We are the Keepers," he said. "We are the Keepers. Waiting."

"Waiting?" the minstrel asked him. "Waiting for what? The Inca's return?"

But the old man did not answer the question. He spoke now to Cusi. "Misti is waiting, and sleep is waiting. Tomorrow's journey is almost upon us."

The boy stumbled to his bed among the sleeping llamas. He was troubled about something, something vague but dimly known. Something that he could not say with words because he did not know them. Something that darkened his heart like a cloud at midday.

A new wind blew low over the ychu grass, crying softly as it swept along. The minstrel was singing again. This time he sang the old, old Inca song that every minstrel knows: "I was born like a lily in a garden."

"Singer of Songs," Cusi murmured sleepily. "Singer of Songs."

5. THE STEEP TRAIL

Cusi needed no one to waken him. He had been awake long before Chuto motioned him to follow along as the Old One walked yesterday's trail to the place of the Sunrise Call. The way did not seem as long this morning as it had the day before, or as difficult, or as dark. Cusi kept within touching distance of Chuto's swiftly moving shadow slipping through the dawn. The boy was pleased that the trail was easier to follow. Just once walking over it and I know it well, he thought. My feet learn quickly, or maybe it's these new sandals Chuto made yesterday. Maybe some of the minstrel's music went into the making. The boy chuckled at the thought, but as Chuto turned his head to listen Cusi stopped his laughter. Perhaps this was not the time for letting thoughts go straying. Perhaps he should be thinking of the Great Sun Father.

Cusi shivered. This morning the wind was very cold. It was filled with the chill breath of the snowbanks. It was not a day wind, loud and lusty. It was a dawn wind of the high sierras, low and slow and cold. Only the sun could warm the world and make it right for living.

The man and the boy had now reached the rock circle and stood waiting, facing the eastern sky. Slowly the sky colored, heralding the coming day. Slowly Cusi felt happiness fill his body warmly. This had never happened to him before. Never before had he felt happiness flowing with his blood to make his body warm and light with captured laughter and delight.

Then the sun came. Chuto's voice rose to meet the sun, and Cusi knew forever the joy of welcoming the coming of the Great Father who lightened and warmed the world.

After the call was finished Chuto stood for a minute with head bowed, lost in thinking. For a brief time he had touched the Spirit World, and he hated to return to the realness of living. But it was only for a moment. With a sigh the old man raised his head, straightened his thin shoulders, and turned to the homeward trail.

The way back was even more swift than the coming had been. Chuto was troubled. Cusi felt it, and he knew what was troubling the Old One. He does not want to leave our llamas. He does not want to see the outside world, the boy thought and felt guilt at his own excitement in going.

Breakfast was quiet. The minstrel sat deep in thought. His face was closed this morning. No flashing smile came to lighten its darkness and to soften its sternness. More than ever he bore the look of an eagle ready for flight. His songs had stilled themselves. His pipes lay silent on the ychu grass. Only his body was with them. His mind and his heart were traveling another trail.

Suncca whined and whined, and the day wind began blowing. Misti kept close beside his young master. Chuto ate, looking only at the food set before them.

Cusi would have liked to talk. He needed to talk. Going to the Salt Pits was an event that needed to be talked about. But the boy did not talk. The silence of the two men was too heavy to cut through with words.

The breakfast corn and potatoes eaten, Chuto began to pack. The minstrel stirred and looked around. Then he spoke.

"Perhaps I know more than my songs," he said. "Perhaps I, too, have been sent along the path I follow. Are you certain, brother, that you want this salt you journey to get? Are you sure it is what you want to do?"

Chuto nodded but did not speak or stop his work of getting the possessions together.

After a time the minstrel spoke again. "Hidden Valley takes care of its flock and the keepers of its flock. Not so the world outside. The outside world is filled with people who are strange to you. They are people of two bloods. They are and they are not. They know and they do not know. They care and they do not care. Think, brother. Are you certain that you want to ford this river of people whose blood runs fresh and salt in never-mixing streams?"

Chuto answered simply, "I do not want to go. There is need to go. It has been asked of me. Once I received a like request and I refused it. The cost of that refusal lies heavy in my heart."

To this the minstrel had no answer. Instead he went into the hut and brought out his pack. "This," he said, handing Chuto a small package, "is food fit for a journey. It is brown sugar and parched corn. Eat it as you walk along and your feet will not stumble because of hunger."

Chuto was pleased. He took the package offered him. "I know this food. I carried it always when I too journeyed over the mountain trails."

Cusi had been whispering to Misti, but now he looked at Chuto in surprise. He had not known that Chuto had traveled the mountain trails. He had never thought about it, really, but if he had he would have thought that Chuto always had lived in Hidden Valley. He felt a flash of jealousy that Chuto had known another world than this they shared together. He must know more about it. All about it. Where had Chuto been?

The boy began a question, but the minstrel stopped him. "Look how pleased Misti is that you are going to see the world beyond the swinging bridge," he said jokingly.

Cusi's eyes danced with delight. "Are we going by the narrow trail? Are we going over the swinging bridge? Is it possible?" he asked. His words tumbled over themselves in his excitement.

Chuto nodded, and the minstel laughed, "Why not? It is the shortest way down the mountain, especially if you should fall." He was teasing now. Cusi laughed with him.

Chuto counted the bundles aloud. "These two rolled mats for sleeping. I take one. One for Cusi. Inside them—so—I put the squares of woven cloth for the salt. The coils of rope to tie them. Two for me and one for Cusi. The gift package of food I will divide. We will need to eat it as we walk along. The extra sandals and the ponchos I will take. The gourds for drinking I tie here to this. The spun yarn for trading goes in Cusi's pack, all except that which we spin as we walk along. It is all here, I think. Yes, it is all here."

Chuto stood up and looked around with satisfaction. It was good to know that everything that was needed was in its place, ready for the taking.

Quickly he rolled the mats. The smaller one was Cusi's. He tied it across the boy's shoulders. The larger one he took upon his own back. Then he tied his coca bag full of dried coca leaves and lime lumps made of seashell to the sash at his side where his poncho opened. The small coca bag he gave to Cusi, who tied it to his own sash. Then the Old One looped his slingshot over his shoulder. It was his only weapon. He was not a hunter; he was a shepherd. The slingshot was all he needed.

They were ready to go. Everything was ready. There was nothing more to do.

They said good-by.

Misti looked after them. His sharp pointed ears with the red woolen tassels stood straight up in surprise. Could it be that he was being left behind? Quietly and deliberately he spat—at nothing in particular, just to show his displeasure. It made him feel better.

Suncca whined. It was the only thing he could do. It did not make him feel better. He whined too much and too often.

Chuto and Cusi had begun their journey. They walked across the meadow of ychu grass, a thin old man and a thinner, younger boy. They were dressed alike, knitted woolen caps of bright llama yarn on their heads, blue ponchos with red embroidered stripes woven of llama wool on their shoulders, white shin-length cotton trousers, and tied llama sandals. Their rolled mat bundles moved as their shoulders moved.

They did not look back. They had begun their journey. They were on their way.

They passed the opening of the llama trail down into the valley where the Indian family were clearing the underbrush for their new home. In a way, Cusi would have liked to take this trail. If they had done so, he could have seen the family close by. He could, perhaps, have talked with them. Then he would have known so much more about them than he possibly could learn just by watching. Also, if they had gone by way of the llama trail, he could have taken Misti. Since Misti had been old enough to leave his mother, Yellow-Ears, he had been the boy's companion by day and by night. Cusi felt strange to be going off without the beautiful black llama walking proudly beside him.

But quickly the young Indian boy forgot Misti in his excitement over the trail they were taking. This trail lay behind the ruins of the stone corral, behind the grass-thatched hut, behind the mountain meadow where the llamas grazed. It was hidden from view by a clump of trees hung heavily with vines and covered thickly with velvet green moss and white feathered lichens.

Cusi knew about this trail, but he had never traveled it before. At once it led steeply a hundred feet downward to the knifelike edge of a sheer rock cliff. Two thousand feet below them tumbled and stormed the roaring rapids of a wide, swiftly moving river. The deep thunder roar of the rapids could be heard distinctly on the cliff crest where Chuto and Cusi stood. Beneath them white spray shot upward like a lacy veil, partly hiding the dark green water of the river and giant tree trunks that were being tossed and splintered against sharp boulders in the mighty current.

The boy lifted his eyes from the wild, angry scene below him and let them travel to the opposite cliff that loomed just as sharply and just as sheer on the far side of the wide, wide river.

Over the gorge, above the rapids, connecting cliff to cliff, swung a slender bridge. This was the swinging bridge the minstrel had teased about. This was the bridge that they must cross.

The bridge was made of rope vines of maguey plant. These vines had been twisted and plaited together into two cables as thick as Chuto's body. They were tied into holes that had been drilled in the cliff walls. Between the rope cables planks had been tied. Higher up was a smaller vine rope to be used as a handrail.

Cusi had looked at this swinging bridge before, but he had

never thought of crossing it. Now terror touched him with its cold fingers, and hot excitement filled him with the thought of what he was about to do. He felt that he never could move a sandaled foot a half-pace forward. Yet he knew that he would move. He knew that he would cross the bridge. He knew that nothing could hinder that first step that would lead forward.

Chuto looked at the boy once, briefly, then stepped upon the first plank. Cusi watched him. He was terrified. He was fascinated. He was at once impatient and yet frightened for his own starting. Step by step, hand by hand, the old man crossed the canyon. The frail-looking bridge swayed and swung. Far below it the rapids leaped upward in icy frenzy.

Chuto became but a small speck moving along the rocking vine cable. Slowly, slowly, slowly he moved farther along. He reached the middle, and the bridge dipped hammock-like. Cusi never took his eyes from the black dot on the slender line. Breathlessly he watched. He waited. He watched.

Ah! Chuto had reached the far cliff ledge. He stood there, gaining his balance on the firm rock cliff!

Then he turned, raising a hand as signal for Cusi's starting.

Not for nothing had Chuto trained the boy to obey his commands. This was reward for his years of patient teaching. Cusi put one foot on the first plank and moved his body forward. He was on the bridge now. He must keep going. Move a foot and move a hand. Inch forward. Never look backward. Never look downward. Never look anywhere but the opposite cliff where good, kind Chuto waited.

Suddenly Cusi was not afraid. He felt bold and brave and strong and tall. This was adventure. This was fun. He was at the middle now. The bridge was not dipping as much as it had done when Chuto crossed. It was swinging. It was swaying. It was rocking, but it was not dipping. Keep going. Keep going. Step by step. Hand by hand. Never look down. Keep looking at Chuto. He was bigger now. Chuto was bigger. He could see him plainly. He was his everyday size.

The bridge stopped moving underfoot. Cusi had reached the firm rock ledge. He had reached the other side. The world danced crazily around him. Around and around. Dizzily he leaned forward. He shut his eyes to clear his dizziness. Chuto said mildly, "A few coca leaves can be chewed now, I think. Yes, we will sit here with our backs against the cliff wall and chew some coca leaves."

Cusi was glad to sit down. He did not look again at the bridge across the chasm. He did not need to see it. He had crossed it. That was enough.

Far below the rapids sprayed and foamed. The dark green river flowed its way through the heart of a mountain made of granite.

A condor soared and swerved and circled in graceful, lazy curves against the tropic sky.

White clouds tore themselves on the jagged crested mountains and hung in gray wisps upon the pointed peaks of deeper, whiter glistening snow.

Chuto stood up, stretching himself, and motioned with his lips that this was the way that they would go. The cliff where they were was a rounded pillar of granite. There was no trail up its smooth, hard sides. There was no trail down.

Cusi watched Chuto as the Indian swung upward, catching the end of a narrow ladder made of tied tree branches. Then he boosted Cusi up so that the boy could catch the ladder ends, could hold them tightly in his hands, could get a foothold on the ladder. Cusi began climbing. He had to climb. He could not get down. There was only space beneath him.

The granite rock was in layers of color, beautiful colors, rich and dark and aged with weather and with years. Cusi dared not look up or down or sideways. There was no Chuto to watch, for the old man had been left far below him.

Across the cliff face the boy climbed steadily. Sweat ran into his eyes, stinging them with its salt. His hands were wet against the ladder rungs.

But he climbed on and on. At last he reached safety behind the granite wall. The mountain here sloped gently into a lush, green valley. Vines and ferns, bushes and flowers and orchid plants made a world more beautiful than a dream. There was no ychu grass or bare, brown hills. Only by looking far, far above in the blue painted sky could he see the pointed peaks of snow.

Below him in the valley a gentle rain was falling. The wetness of the raindrops made the greenness of the jungle fresher, greener, and more vivid.

"Hidden Valley lies behind us." Cusi turned at the sound. Chuto was jumping lightly from the top of the ladder to the sloping trail.

6. THE LONG WAY

The Indian untied the gourd drinking cups, and he and the boy drank mountain water from a crystal pool. They bathed their faces in its coolness and rested in the shade, munching the minstrel's gift of parched and caked brown sugar. The sun was high in the sky. There were no shadows. It was midday.

In about an hour the man and the boy started down the mountain trail. They walked slowly. This was a new world for Cusi. Everything was strange and interesting to the boy. Chuto was patient and kind. He explained everything. He knew the names of the flowers and gathered a handful to show the boy. There were purple columbine and purple munca flowers. There were the yellow-white dead-man's-shoes and the golden-yellow teardrops-of-the-sun. He gathered bunches of punga-punga. These flowers he would dry and use as medicine when they returned to their Hidden Valley.

He showed the boy tracks of the puma, mountain lion, and of atoc, the fox. By a fern-clad streamlet they found the heart-shaped hoofprints of the small deer of the Andes.

The air was hot and heavy and thick and difficult to breathe. Cusi felt slow and stupid and sleepy. He had never felt like this in the thin, cold air of the mountaintops. The air, too, was sweet with flower scent and dank with the smell of tree mold and earth mold. There was no wind, no movement of any kind.

The jungle kept its own secrets in the green silences of its shaded depths.

Chuto named the trees for Cusi. Eucalyptus from Australia, willow and poplar brought from Europe. The trees and their names and the countries they came from meant nothing to Cusi. They were strange to sight and sound. They left no memory in his mind, no echo in his heart. He saw them. That was all.

By midafternoon they had begun climbing again. Chuto hurried. "We must get to the crest before evening falls," he explained to Cusi. "We have friends yonder. Do you see their clearing away up the mountain slope, a tiny patch of brown?"

Cusi looked, but he saw no brown—only green, every shade of green and every hue of green. His eyes ached with the unfamiliar color. Even in closing them, green seeped through his squinted lids. He was so sleepy. His feet felt heavy and as if they did not belong to him. "My feet are two heavy somethings that I pick up and put down and pick up and put down," he told Chuto.

Chuto laughed. "It is because we are in lower country. You must remember that our home is thousands of feet above us."

Cusi was interested. He had not thought about altitude before. He had not needed to think about it. In the world he knew everything was high or higher. "Is low altitude what makes it so warm and so green and so thick with plants and trees?" he asked.

Chuto nodded. "Partly," he said. "But save your breath for climbing. I feel safer in the mountains at nighttime than in the jungle valley. Besides, there are several places we must cross while there is light enough to see our footing."

"Are there more bridges or more ladders?" Cusi wanted to know.

"No," Chuto told him, "but the trail is rocky and steep and there may have been landslides."

Cusi knew about landslides. They had them often in the highlands. He had seen tons and tons of snow and earth and boulders slide down a mountain slope, taking trees and rocks and whatever living thing was in the path of its sliding. He hurried his steps to match Chuto's. He knew about mountain slides. He agreed with Chuto that when darkness fell he would feel safer on the mountain crest than deep in this valley walled with green.

Soon they came to several scattered huts in a small clearing. A woman was threshing pigweed by the door of the largest hut. On a square of blanket on the ground she had placed the canihua stalks. With a wooden flail she was beating them. She stopped when she saw strangers on the trail and called to someone within the hut. A boy about Cusi's age came to the door and silently stared at the two visitors. Chuto asked for water, and the boy brought two gourds of cool fresh spring water. At a word from the woman he went again into the hut and brought out goat's milk, yellow and rich and warm. Cusi tasted the milk from the gourd handed him, but he did not like it. He handed the gourd to Chuto and drank more of the cool spring water. It tasted better. Besides, he knew what it was. He would have liked to talk to the boy, but shyness overcame his desire. The woman asked, not looking at them, where they were going and from whence they had come. Chuto pointed backward over the trail they had come and said, "We come from the highlands. We travel to the Salt Pits." That was all. There seemed nothing else to say. Chuto thanked them for the refreshments, and he and Cusi started on the trail again. The boy and the woman watched them go. They saw no one else in the clearing. Soon all trace of it was swallowed in the dense green background.

The trail grew steep and rocky. At times they went up narrow stone steps. Once they came to a gigantic boulder. Cusi looked upward worriedly. He could see no ladder. As they approached the immense rock, Chuto turned abruptly. They entered a low, narrow, winding tunnel. It was as black as night and felt damp and clammy. Smell of wet earth, so thick it left Cusi panting, hung heavy throughout the long way. Cusi felt relief when suddenly they were in sunlight again. The mountains now were bare and bleak and brown. A steady wind blew against them, making the going difficult. Night was coming across the highlands. The sun with its warmth and light was gone. It had not lingered to paint the sky in memory of its passing. It just was gone, sinking its brilliancy quickly in the soft lush green beneath them.

Another stairway, a trail on a crest where straight down on either side there was nothing but space, filled now with the purple shadows of night.

Cusi smelled fire smoke before he saw it. He knew that smell—llama dung. How homelike, how good, how safe it smelled! High on the brown, bare mountain they came to an ancient ruin. On a cliff crest were the walls of stone, and up to it, across terraces, up stairways, through arches the travelers plodded wearily.

Chuto began to shout, "Ay—e, Ay—e, Ay—e," and the brown mountains called back, "Ah–y—e, Ah–y—e, Ah–y—e," in echoed refrain.

Two men and several women and three or four children

appeared as if by magic. The men raised their hands in glad salute. They called a warm welcome. They knew Chuto. They were friends.

"Welcome to Condor Kuncca," the older man said, meeting Chuto at the foot of the last terrace. "What brings our brother to us?" he asked and continued, "Whatever it is, we are honored by the visit." Then he added, placing a kind hand on Cusi's shoulder, "This one, of course, is one of the Chosen! The other one did not return?"

Chuto replied, "Death has no returning. Yes, this time a good choice, I think."

Cusi looked at him. Why is it, he wondered, that Chuto talks in riddles to other men, but to me, Cusi, his words are simple and plain. However, the Indian seemed to understand. He was smiling at Chuto and nodding his head. They shook hands.

Chuto spoke again. "A man learns, I think, with the passing of his days. This time I myself open the gate. If it is closed, his hand, not mine, shall close it."

They had reached the stone building now. The younger Indian came forward to shake Chuto's hand in welcome and to welcome also the young boy with him. The women were shy. They laughed behind their hands, but Cusi knew that was their way. No one had told him, but he understood that a welcome does not need to be expressed by words or gestures. If the heart speaks to the stranger, the stranger feels at home.

Cusi was interested in the stone building at the top of the terraces and stairways. The younger Indian sensed his interest and said, "Perhaps you wonder why we call this Condor Kuncca? But see, is it not like an eagle's nest here on the crest of a rock cliff?"

Cusi looked and nodded. It was like an eagle's nest. It was

like home too. He knew this stonework; it was the masterpiece of ancient builders. He knew the smell of the smoke; it was llama dung. These men were herdsmen.

Presently he saw the llamas. There were perhaps a dozen of them resting by the shelter of the stone corrals. He wondered why there were not more. There were hundreds in his flock at Hidden Valley.

The women went in to prepare the evening meal. They had a different kind of food from what Cusi had at home. They had roasted guinea pig and sweet potatoes. Cusi was hungry. He liked the taste of this food.

The children were small and were afraid of strangers. They hid in the wide skirts of their mothers. Cusi could see only their big black eyes watching him, watching him, watching him.

When the men had finished eating, the women and the children disappeared within the shelter. The men were left by the fire to sip chicha and talk. Cusi tried to listen, but their words were strange. He did not understand their meaning. He was tired. Unrolling his sleeping mat, he curled up in the shelter of the wall. Chuto put the extra poncho over him, but the tired young boy did not know it. He was asleep.

40330

7. QUESTIONS

The next morning, directly after sunrise, they left. The women had given them packages of dried meat and dried sweet potatoes. The men had given Chuto a gourd of chicha to carry with him. Now they stood on the top terrace, waving to them —the men, the women, and even the children. They were so friendly. Cusi looked back at them and smiled and waved. Now that he was going, his shyness had left him. He called good-by.

Chuto was far on the trail. Cusi hastened to overtake him. He could hear the lead llama bell tinkling merrily as the llamas began their morning grazing. Cusi called good-by to them in passing.

The mountain on this far side was not steep. There was no swinging bridge to cross nor frail ladder to climb. I know why we call our valley Hidden Valley, the boy thought. The mountains hide it so well. It's almost as if no one is supposed to find it.

The trail led through an open meadow. Chuto pointed out a hacienda in the distance. It was a long, low building of brown adobe mud. It had a sloping roof of bright red tile. As they came nearer, they could see its many doorways and other openings. Chuto called these openings windows, and explained their use to the highland boy.

The hacienda was enclosed by a low mud wall. There was a blue gate in the wall. Cusi looked over it and saw a patio filled with growing flowers of many colors.

At the back of the low adobe building were green fields sloping down to a lazy river. Men were working the fields with oxen, huge white, slow-moving, patient beasts. They kept their great heads lowered, looking at the ground and never at the sun. They seemed to say, "We have been conquered. We have nothing to hope for." Looking at them made Cusi sad. They were so big, so dull, so broken.

The trail widened into a roadway paved with cobblestones. The stones were rounded and smooth, polished for centuries by passing feet, animal feet and feet of men their masters.

Men were on the road now. Most of them were walking, but some were riding small brown burros. The burros were not at all like the oxen. They were small and frisky and saucy and gay. Cusi laughed at the funny burrows whose long ears seemed too big for them to manage. He laughed again when he saw women riding sidesaddle on the fat brown donkeys. The women did not mind. They laughed back at him and called to him in a tongue he did not know.

"Do these people in this country not know how to say words of intelligence?" he asked Chuto in surprise.

It was Chuto's turn to laugh. "They know how to talk. It is you who do not know how to listen," he teased the boy.

Cusi was indignant, and Chuto stopped teasing to explain. "These are Spanish people. They are not Indian. Their words are Spanish words, not Indian," he said. "Perhaps I should teach you Spanish. Yes, that is what I should do. Perhaps."

"Do you speak Spanish?" Cusi asked. "I have not heard you."

Chuto laughed shortly. "With whom would I speak? The llamas know Indian."

Chuto pointed to a nearby field where people were planting. "There are some Indians," he said. "The people of the hacienda and those who work the oxen and ride on burros are not Indian. They are Spanish."

"Why don't they have llamas instead of burros?" Cusi asked. "Llamas are better."

The old man answered proudly, "No one who has a drop of blood not Indian can manage a llama. The llama remembers," he added darkly.

In the potato field a long line of men were working. Each man had a long-handled spade with a foothold tied to it. They worked together and in rhythm. At the call of the leader each man jumped upward with a shout. Then they came down together, plunging the sharp spade points into the earth of the field. Kneeling on the earth before them was a long line of women. As the men dug the earth the women turned it with their strong brown hands.

Cusi would have liked to stay a long time watching the people working. Chuto was impatient. Their journey was almost at an end. He wanted to get there, to get the salt and to go home again.

At the ruins of the Sacred Baths of the Inca they rested. They bathed in the cold water that bubbled in a spring and came from the melted snows of the high sierras. Chuto told Cusi to sit in the high throne seat carved from solid rock. It was where the Inca had sat in the long ago when the Inca was mighty ruler of a vast and loyal kingdom. Now a young boy sat there and pulled thoughtfully at his golden earplugs. Was he of the ancient nobility? Was that what the minstrel had meant when he and Chuto talked together? Did the royal blood of ancient kings still flow in the veins of his people? Again Cusi felt a vague unknown trouble like a cloud over the sun of a happy day. Again he felt a longing in his heart. Was it for kinship? Was it for family? How could he miss what he had not known?

Chuto too seemed troubled. He sat on a rock seat above the babbling spring that lay in its carved basin of pure white stone. He did not seem impatient now to meet whatever lay before him. He seemed rather to be going backward into days that were gone. "You are old for your age, my Cusi, and wise, too, I think. Wiser than I when I had your years. Wiser perhaps than that other who chose another way."

Cusi could feel his heart beat wildly as he listened to the words Chuto was saying to him. There had been someone else, then. Had it been another boy? Cusi wondered. What had happened to this other one? Where was he now? Cusi decided to find out. He said, "You speak of someone that I do not know. What other one do you talk about?"

Chuto got to his feet. He answered hurriedly, "Not now. Not now. My heart does not say that this is the time to tell you things that some day you must know." He looked around worriedly for something new to talk about. Pointing to a distant opening between the faraway mountain peaks, he said, "In that direction Cuzco lies—Cuzco the Holy City, divided into four parts by three rivers, and from its heart four great roads lead to the four corners of the world that is Peru." The old man looked at the boy to see if he were listening, to see if he were interested. He tried again. "Four roads there were in the days of the Inca: to the mountains, to the valleys, to the pampas, to the sea."

But Cusi felt stubborn. "Why do you know these things? Where did you learn them? Why do you never tell me what I want to know? Chuto, respected one, tell me who I am."

The old man looked pleadingly at the boy seated above him. "I must be sure that you have understanding before I speak. Bear with me, my Cusi," he said softly. "I do the best I know."

Cusi was embarrassed. He felt ashamed of his fretful questions. Chuto's words made him feel uneasy. What Chuto must tell him, he must be ready to hear. He could learn to wait.

He jumped from the Inca seat where he had been sitting. He flashed a quick smile at the worried Old One, who smiled in return in fondness and in gratitude.

Glad of an opportunity to change their conversation, both Indians, the old one and the young one, turned away from the ruins of the Inca Bath and onto the trail again.

They walked along in silence, a comfortable silence. They were companions. Companions have no need for constant talking.

8. OUTSIDE

It was not long before the two Indians entered the Valley of the Salt. This too had been used in ancient times and was still being used in much the same manner. The Valley of the Salt was a wide, open, flat valley, terraced in sections by low walls made of perfectly fitted stone.

Here and there in the terraces men could be seen, working busily in the hot sun of afternoon. They dug shallow holes in the loose grainy soil. These were filled shortly with water from some underground source. Chuto, who knew so many things, did not know just what it was that caused this water to be salty. But salty it was, and it was this sandy, salty brine that the men scooped out of the shallow holes into hollowed stone traylike vessels that were lying about in great numbers. Under the hot tropical sun it would not be many hours before the water evaporated. The coarse, gray, sandy salty substance that remained was the salt they used.

When Chuto and Cusi arrived at the pits they spent no time resting. They began working immediately. Chuto dug the shallow holes. Cusi dipped the salt brine into the stone trays.

The sun burned down in glaring fierceness. When Cusi would have stopped, Chuto pointed to the boy's coca bag. "Chew some," he ordered briefly. "We must get our supply today so that it will be dry enough to take tomorrow." Cusi was glad that they would not stay long at this place. He liked it even less than he had the wooded jungle places they had seen yesterday.

The coca he chewed made him feel less tired. He bent to his task again. After another hour of working the sun sank below the distant hills. For a short time it was breathlessly hot. Then the night wind came over the flat land, bringing sharp, stinging cold. Chuto helped Cusi finish scooping the sandy brine into the trays. Then they went over to join the other salt diggers, who had stopped work also and were now sitting around a small supper fire.

Chuto brought the yarn he had carried down the mountain to barter. While they ate parched corn and dried meat, Chuto bargained. The other men examined the yarn, noting its quality and the evenness of its spinning. "The women of your village spin good yarn," one man told him. Chuto did not answer. He did not say there were no women in his village. He did not say he had no village. He did not say that he had spun the yarn and under his patient teaching Cusi had spun some of it. Although spinning is chiefly women's work, men and boys know how to spin. Occasionally they can be seen spinning yarn as they walk along the highland trails.

But Chuto said none of this. He merely looked pleased, and the men took that for answer. The women of his village were good spinners. That was what they thought. Chuto let them think it. He was a good bargainer. Cusi was proud of him as the value of the yarn went up and up. When the trading was finished everyone was pleased. Chuto had a pile of peanuts and a stack of dried fish. The men had yarn spun evidently by a village of expert weavers.

Besides, bargaining was fun. It eased the strangeness of

meeting. It gave them something to talk about. Each man showed his wits, his cleverness, and his smartness. It made for laughter. It gained respect. These men knew one another now as men of similar abilities. They were acquainted. Now they could talk together of many things.

At the opposite side of the valley a narrow steep road led into the sloping hills. Along this road there now appeared two round glaring eyes. They would appear and disappear and appear again, each time rounder, more glaring, larger. Cusi was terrified. It must be an animal from another world. He looked fearfully at the men, but in the gathering dusk he could not see their faces plainly. They did not seem frightened. He could not feel their fear. They were leaning forward, watching the lights, but more in expectancy and interest than in fear. The lights came nearer and nearer with strange noise and a still stranger smell. Then they disappeared completely. The men waited. Cusi saw two men walking across the gray-blanketed terraces.

Chuto chuckled, looking down at Cusi's set face. "Come," he said to the boy. "Come with me. We will see what this thing is that comes with such a clamor." Cusi made himself follow the old Indian across the terraces to the beginning of the road.

"They call this thing a truck," Chuto explained. "It has wheels instead of feet. It has a motor instead of a heart. It has evil-smelling blood by name of gasoline." Chuto knew everything!

When Cusi could get his breath, he asked, "What pulls it? Where are its eyes? It had them open. I saw them." Chuto laughed and quietly, patiently explained the mysteries of a thing that lived and moved but was not alive. It took a while. Cusi was not one to believe merely because he saw it. He must understand.

Chuto sighed. The world outside of Hidden Valley was so strange, so fascinating, so full of interest and of wonder, so very big. This was what he had been dreading, but it was why he had come. He knew what Cusi was experiencing. Had it not happened to him? Had it not happened to that other one? It happened to each in his lifetime. It must happen. It was the law. And each reacted to it in his own way. That too was a part of the pattern. Chuto sighed again and again explained the mystery and the magic of this thing here before them that they could see and touch.

By and by they returned to the group. The supper fire was completely dead. Fuel was too scarce to burn for pleasure or for warmth. It was gathered slowly. It was hoarded carefully. It was burned frugally and only when necessary.

The men were bartering with the newcomers, the men of the truck. This truck was full of coca leaves for the highland markets. They had come from the eastern slopes of the Andes, where coca is grown. In between their trading talk they told of other things. They told about coca-growing. How it grows only in the wettest lands, how it grows in low, small bushes and must be lovingly tended. They told of the skill and care needed in picking the leaves four times each year. They explained how it was dried and packed in woven net bags. "Eighteen pounds to the bag," they said, "no more, no less."

From coca-growing to other things the talk lazily drifted into the wind and into the night.

One of the men had come up from the fishing villages on the seacoast. He had dried fish to trade along the way to the

market at Cuzco. Cusi listened wide-eyed to his tales of
the sea. The man described the waves of a storm-swept sea to
be as high as mountain peaks. Cusi tried to picture mountains
of water pointing up to the sky, but he couldn't do it. A bottom-
less pool of still, black water, a swirling river cutting its way
through granite, white foaming rapids breaking trees into
splinters—these things he could picture. He had seen them in
life. He could see them in memory. But mountains of water,
rolling and tossing and pitching on a sea of water, he could not
imagine. Finally he gave up and sat listening to the tales, en-
tertained but unbelieving.

He did not remember sleeping, but he must have slept. He
wakened in the gray dawn, cramped and cold. The men were
where he had left them, huddled around a tiny fire. Only this
was morning. This was breakfast fire. The men were eating
again, but this morning no one talked. Last night they had
shared talk and experiences; this morning each was bent upon
his own individual task.

Chuto thought it would take an hour more of sunshine to dry
the salt enough for packing. It took longer. It was midday before they were packed and on the trail again.

Just before they departed, two men and a boy about Cusi's
age came to the pits. The two boys eyed each other and would
have liked to talk and get acquainted. Cusi thought, I think I
like that boy. I wish he lived in Hidden Valley. I could show
him Misti. But there was no time to break down shyness, nor
even to speak.

The boy was scooping brine from the holes the men dug
when Cusi went by him, packed with salt to take the homeward trail. The boy looked up, and his eyes met Cusi's. They
were not Indian eyes; they were Spanish eyes. He could not

talk with me even if there was time, Cusi thought. He would not know my Indian language. Never in my whole life have I talked with a boy, Cusi thought with despair. He looked back once, but the boy was bent over the salt hole, dipping salt brine.

It was night again when they arrived at Condor Kuncca, the Indian shelter. Cusi had thought that surely this time he could make friends with the small children there. But they were asleep. In a clay bed not much larger than a shelf they were rolled in little knots, noisily sleeping. Cusi looked at them. How cunning they were, and little and brown. Brothers and sisters! Family!

The boy slept again near the llama corral while Chuto and the other men talked.

Early next morning they were far along the trail before the sun rose and Chuto put down his pack to greet it with his ancient prayer.

The way home was uneventful. There was no one at all at the hut where the woman had been threshing pigweed. The place had a lonely, unfriendly look. Cusi was glad when Chuto did not stop.

It was midafternoon when they reached the place of the tree-tied ladder. Cusi was surprised when Chuto put down his pack and prepared to stay. The boy had thought that if they hurried they could be home not too long after dark. He could see Misti and Yellow-Ears and the rest of the flock. He could hear Suncca whine. He could tell the minstrel all the things that had happened on the journey. He could be home for the night. Now that he was so close he wanted to go on, to be really home again.

Chuto said, "No," and then to the boy's look of disappointment added, "The swinging bridge needs not the shadows of evening but the brightness of day for its crossing."

Cusi was not pleased. He set his pack down with a thud. He sat himself down and wound his arms around his knees and tried to see around the cliff and along the trail and over the rapids to home.

Home. What a wonderful place it was. He would never leave it again, or if he did it would be for a short time only.

Chuto sighed. "Is your heart going back over the trail your feet have traveled?" he asked tiredly.

Cusi shook his head. "That way," he said, pointing his lips on the way toward home. Chuto laughed, and his laughter held the precious tones of gladness.

9. AMAUTA COMES

After a week of being home again Cusi had difficulty in making himself believe he had ever been outside Hidden Valley. He would sit in the meadow watching his flock to see that no harm came to them and think over and over and over all that had happened lately. He would put the things in order carefully: the family coming to the valley below, the minstrel coming, walking the swinging bridge over the roaring rapids, climbing the ladder across the cliff face, crawling through the narrow dark tunnel, the jungle trail, the family at Condor Kuncca, the Inca Baths, the Salt Pit, and all that he had seen and heard while he was there.

He strung them along on a string of thinking, each happening a knot on the string, each knot a memory.

He remembered so vividly. He remembered every movement, every color, every feeling, every sound. But it was a dream remembered. It must not have happened. It could not have happened. It was a part of a world that never was.

Cusi would come up from the depths of his dreaming to look around. He saw the mountains crowded close together to hide, to guard his valley. He saw the pointed snow peaks above the ragged clouds. He saw the snow fields, their white flatness sparkling with iridescent lights. He saw the clusters of stunted, misshapen trees and the sharp, outjutting boulders. He saw the stone corral and the grass-thatched roof of his shelter. He saw the moss-green ychu grass and the llamas grazing.

This was reality. This was fact. This was the world he lived in. These were the things he could touch and smell. These were the things he could hear and see. These were the things that were real.

Only in memory could he see the foaming rapids tossing their crystal spray. Only in memory could he smell the heavy rich earth mold smell of the jungle trail. Only in memory could he hear the minstrel's songs and the pipes of Pan.

Cusi sighed. More than anything he missed the minstrel. It was so sadly silent now that he had gone. Chuto was quiet these days. He was kind. He was patient. He was always near to show and to help, but he talked so little. Did Chuto miss the world outside of Hidden Valley? Did he miss the minstrel's song? Cusi asked himself these questions, but only the whining of the timid Suncca and the humming of the llamas answered him.

Soon it was shearing time. The boy was glad of the activity. He was glad for something to do. He was glad of the roughness and the toughness of the world each day and the tiredness of his body as he crawled to sleep each night.

The two Indians worked from gray dawn to gray dusk. It takes two to shear a llama. Llamas resent being sheared. Chuto would throw, then hold, a llama flat on its side. Cusi's work was to cut short, but not too short, the matted, coarse outside hair and the long silky hair next to the llama's body. The boy used an old-fashioned shepherd's knife, and it was very dull. He had to stop often to whet it on nearby stones. Then he had to cut faster than ever because Chuto could not hold the llama down for long. One side sheared, Cusi and Chuto would turn the llama over. Cusi would sharpen his knife and shear some more. Then another llama would be caught and thrown and sheared, and another and another.

Sometimes while he was shearing Cusi would have time to look at the animal he was working on. He would look at it with affection and with pride. Like all Indians of the Andes highlands, he loved the graceful beasts. They were his friends, his companions, and his burden-bearers. They gave him his sandals, his cap, his poncho, and his blanket. They gave him his textile bags and his rawhide net bags, his rope and his slingshot. They gave him fuel for his fire and blood for his ancient sacrifice. They were a part of his past and his present, his everyday and his spiritual existence.

Chuto pointed out the narrow, two-toed feet, each toe having its separate pad which enabled the animal to be sure-footed in climbing. "They were created for us," Chuto told the wondering boy, "created for highland people. For twelve thousand years they have served us."

Cusi had a question. This time he was determined that he would ask it. "Old One"—he spoke hesitantly—"Old One, tell me, how do you know so many things? Where did you learn these things that you tell me?"

Chuto answered simply, "I was taught them, Cusi. Do you think that the keeping of llamas such as these is the work of a simple-minded man?" Then he added with a twinkle in his kind old eyes, "Or of idle men? Come, the year grows late. The llamas must be sheared."

Finally shearing was completed. The fleece was sorted as to color, texture, and length of hair, and piled loosely in bundles for storing. Some of it they would trade. Some of it they would spin into yarn to be woven into caps and ponchos, blankets and squares for bundle wrapping. Some of it, although Cusi did not realize it, would be mysteriously spirited away. To whom? By whose orders? Ah, the answers to these questions were blanketed in mystery.

Cusi had done his work well, and Chuto showed his pride in him. "What did you do last year and all the years when I was too young to help you?" Cusi wanted to know.

Chuto replied, "Your mind is like a startled deer drinking at a mountain pool. You jump and leap and bound and splash the water. Do you not know that to quench a thirst drink must be taken slowly and with satisfaction?"

"And not muddy the water." Cusi chuckled.

Chuto answered with serious concern, "There is grave danger of that, Cusi."

In the days that followed, Cusi often thought of what Chuto had said. The boy knew that his mind was thirsty. He knew, too, that muddied water is unfit to drink.

Meanwhile he watched the family in the valley below. Chuto watched them also. They worked and rested and rested and worked and did not seem to know that an old man and a young boy watched them every day.

After they had rested from their weeks of shearing, Chuto said it was time to train Misti as a burden-bearer. This was Misti's fourth year. It was time he learned to serve his master, not just to play with him.

Long ago when Chuto had given Misti to Cusi, he had explained that all of Yellow-Ears' black or silver babies were to belong to the boy. Misti had been the first black one, but now there was another black baby almost old enough to be turned into the flock outside the stone corral.

Yellow-Ears had never given the flock a silver llama baby,

but Cusi knew that some day she would. A silver llama is a wonderful thing to own. It brings health and luck and peace and happiness to its master.

There was a silver llama in the flock now, stately and proud and respected by the other llamas. It did not belong to Cusi. It knew Cusi only as the shepherd boy who tended the flock.

But Cusi did not care. Some day he would own a silver llama, and meanwhile he had the new little black one and the older, larger, proud beautiful black one that was Misti.

Misti was Cusi's companion and had been since the day he had been driven out of his mother's corral. He loved the boy and understood him. Now Cusi began to train him as a burden-bearer.

Chuto instructed the boy in making a loosely woven net bag of rawhide thongs. Then Cusi plaited rope of llama yarn. Everything that Misti needed must belong to Misti and not to any other llama and it must have been made by Misti's master. Cusi bunched the matted, coarse hair on Misti's back to make a padding for the burden.

Then he said softly, "Come, llama. Come, llama. I will load you." Cusi thought he knew all about llamas and all about Misti. He had something new to learn. Misti was just like other llamas. He would not be loaded alone. No, Señor! He would not have it. Finally, Cusi herded seven other llamas with him, gently and by soft words so as not to rouse their dispositions. Misti liked this. He stood quietly in the circle with the others. He turned his head inward when they did and waited for the net bag pack to be tied to his back with the new, soft llama rope.

Then trouble started. Cusi knew that no llama would allow himself to be overloaded. But the other llamas were old and knew better. How was Misti to know what was a load and what was not a load? Cusi put more frozen potatoes in the pack to see what would happen. Misti sat down! The other seven llamas sat down! They turned their heads to look at Cusi with surprise and disapproval.

Cusi's feelings were hurt. He had not believed that Misti would do that to him. He coaxed the proud black llama. He begged him to get up. He flattered him. Then Cusi spoke sternly. He asked Misti if he did not remember their years of being together, and he told the llama that he loved him, but that he, Cusi, was the master.

Then Cusi stepped back, waiting for Misti's answer. He had not long to wait. Misti's answer was immediate and emphatic. He spat! Cusi sadly took the extra weight from Misti's back. Misti got up, and the other seven also rose to their feet. They became gentle and patient again. Misti shook his tasseled ears in llama laughter.

Cusi said nothing. He looked quickly to see if Chuto was watching him. Chuto was. Even Suncca was watching, crouched by a sharp rock, his head on his paws.

"That dog! He is so busy watching me having trouble he has forgotten to whine," Cusi said fiercely to himself. He was irritated and cross. He turned to Chuto to say something, anything that would put an end to the quiet watching. His words were stopped before he spoke them.

They were stopped by a long, low call. It came from the foot trail that led to the swinging bridge. Llamas and dog and boy and man looked up, startled and disbelieving. The call came again, long and low and musical. Tensely, silently, they waited.

The call came a third time and with it, walking into view, came a tall, powerful, kingly figure. The man was Indian, strong and fierce and proud and beautiful. His hair was shoulder-length, as glossy and shining black as a raven's wing. Around his head he wore a turban with a yellow fringe. And his ears—Cusi could not believe what he saw! In his ears were golden earplugs like the ones the boy wore, but these were so large and so heavy they made the man's earlobes hang down halfway to his shoulders.

At once Cusi sensed that this was no ordinary man. This man was of royal blood. He walked with the walk of kings. Cusi turned to see how Chuto would welcome this noble stranger to their highland home. The old man was standing straight and firm, and Cusi was struck by the similarity of their appearance. Chuto was no shepherd of the back country to bow and cringe before a lordly guest. He stepped forward now to greet his visitor.

"I am Amauta, the wise one, the teacher," the stranger said, and his voice was like his call, low and long-sounding and full of music.

Chuto answered him, and his voice also had taken on new melody. "I know," he said, "but it is not time that you come. He is too young. He is too young."

"He is old beyond his years," the stranger told him. "It is ordered."

Chuto bowed his head. "It is ordered," he said with dignity and acceptance. Turning to Cusi, he placed his hand on the young boy's shoulders. "I cannot stay time or alter the pattern of the Ancients. My Cusi, this is Amauta who has come to train you in the things that you should know. Your mind is in his keeping. Your acts obey only the voice of your own heart's whisper."

Chuto turned and walked across the ychu grass. Cusi looked into the deep, grave eyes of the stranger who had come to teach him. The boy felt neither fear nor excitement. All this had happened before. It must have happened, because it was what he had been waiting for and he was ready.

10. A MISSION UNSHARED

Cusi was restless. The Amauta had gone, and the days trailed across the ychu grass without meaning and without end. Cusi did not miss the Amauta as he had missed the minstrel. The Amauta had never laughed with him or teased him or made jokes. The Amauta was just and patient and majestic. He was stern and wise, but he was not gay and fun-loving. He was a friend, but not a companion. Cusi did not miss him as a person, but he missed the fullness of the days the teacher had given him.

Cusi was not happy now that the Amauta had gone. He had liked the training he had undergone. He had liked the knowledge he had gathered. He had liked the new feeling of maturity he had gained and his new size and his new strength, for his body had grown as well as his mind.

But the boy's heart was not at peace. There was something that he wanted that he did not have.

He had learned the history of his Ancients, but he had not learned the story of his own family. He had learned the tribal secrets, but he did not know why he was a shepherd boy in a hidden valley. He knew the lives of the Inca of old, their names and their deeds, but no one told him why they called him "Cusi," an Inca name.

Besides history of his race, plant lore, herb medicine, and the secrets of the stars, he had been taught the use of the quipu.

He could recite glibly to Chuto how, in the days before the first Inca, the people had begun to write symbols for words on the broad leaves of lowland trees. The gods had been angered at this knowledge and so to please the gods the people used the quipu cord.

Cusi had his own quipu cord and he had learned to use it as a calculator, as a memory string, as a record. He knew the meaning of the colors of its twisted threads, red for war, and white for peace, and yellow for the sun, and gold for the sun's tears, and maize for the sun's gift to the world. Cusi could add and subtract and multiply and divide on his quipu as swiftly as the lightning strikes and as sure as the coming of day.

The boy learned his lessons well.

But there were things he had not learned. There were questions that stalked his days and haunted his night dreams. Who was he? Where had he come from? Had he no mother, no family as other boys have? Chuto was kind to him, but he had never called him son. Who was his father?

Before he had gone away across the swinging bridge, the Amauta had given Cusi the traditional thirty-day examination. The boy had passed it easily and with honor. Day by day the feats of memory and of strength and of endurance had become longer and more difficult. Day by day Cusi had accomplished what had been expected of him. He could recite the boundaries, the provinces, and the roads of the ancient kingdom. He could recite the names of the Incas, their days and their deeds. He knew the secrets and the signs and the magic of the Old Ones. He could wrestle and box. He could run swiftly and for great distances. He could endure hardships. He could fast from food and from water for long periods of time.

The Amauta was pleased. Here was a boy who had passed

the examination of royalty in a manner fitting a boy of royal blood! Before he had gone, he had given Cusi the fringed turban that the ancient nobles wore. He had put heavier earplugs of gold in the boy's ears. He had said, "I have taught you all that I know and you have repaid my teaching. You know the rites of your people. You know their ceremonies and their curing powers. Your body and your mind are strong and clean and healthy. I have trained them well. Your heart will direct them." Then the wise man said a strange thing. He said, "Your heart will command your mind and your body. Your heart is good and brave because these many years it has been in the strong hands of Chuto, beloved of the Ancients who command him." Chuto's lips quivered as he heard these words, but otherwise no flicker of movement creased the stillness of his face. Cusi looked at him, and it was then that he noted the Old One's scarred earlobes. Had Chuto, too, once worn the golden earplugs? Why did he not wear them now?

The Amauta was speaking again. "Your heart, my boy, belongs to you. What its commands will be I do not know, nor have I need to know. My work with you is done."

So saying, the teacher had gone, leaving only memory to trail across the ychu grass. Only memory and questions without answers.

Cusi spent longer and longer times in gazing at the family in the valley below. The mother, the father, the children—so busy and so content and so together! Seeing them increased the boy's longing for a family to belong to. Perhaps he had no family. Perhaps he had never had one. But he could find a new one! Could he? But of course! The world outside was full of families. He had seen them on the journey to the Salt Pits. What would it be like to have a mother and father, to have brothers and sisters? The boy's longing grew. He could not put it away; nor could he put it behind him. Daily it walked beside him.

Chuto also spent hours now looking at the family in the lower valley. Finally he seemed satisfied with all that he had seen. He said to Cusi, "Yes, they are deserving. They are the ones, I think, to get this season's gift." He looked at Cusi. "They are right, don't you think, for a mark of favor?" At Cusi's nod the old man continued, "It is families such as these that must be kept independent if the blood of the People is to flow without end." Cusi waited for the Old One to say more, but Chuto seemed satisfied to let the conversation end.

The next morning, shortly after the Sunrise Call, the man said to the boy, "You are old enough now to help me choose them."

Cusi was pleased and excited. Now Chuto will talk with me, he thought. He will tell me why he gives llamas away each year.

Chuto went among the llamas, running his hands expertly over their bodies. He could not see beneath their long hair, but he could feel if the bone formation was a good one, if the flesh was firm. Although the flock was very large, the man and the boy knew each llama as an individual. They knew each one by his traits and his personality. Chuto selected several, then he nodded for Cusi to choose some. Cusi did as the old man had done, feeling the llama's body quickly and with deft fingers. Then he stepped back to squint at his choice to see if it was perfectly proportioned. A good llama is as tall as he is long. Next, Cusi looked at each one's feet and each one's mouth.

Finally he selected three grown ones and a two-year-old.

Chuto was pleased with the selection of the older llamas but shook his head at the choice of the younger one. "No," he told the boy. "We cannot trust people we know so little about to train a young llama as a burden-bearer. Poor training can ruin one." Cusi looked over at Misti, who was never very far from his loved master. Even during the long, exhausting days of the boy's study and training with the Amauta, Chuto had not allowed him to neglect his training of Misti. Now Misti was as perfectly trained as any llama in the flock. He obeyed the softest command. He carried his loads with care and with pride. Of course Cusi could laugh now at the memory. Misti had never been overloaded but once. That time Misti trained me, Cusi thought, sending a smile toward Chuto. Chuto smiled back. He knew what the boy was thinking. It was a joke they shared, unspoken.

Chuto said, "Choose all of them. There will be twelve, I think. Yes, a family such as that one will share a gift. You choose the remainder, Cusi. Your judgment is as good as mine."

Cusi laughed. Praise from Chuto made any day a happy one.

He began running toward the corral of the mother llamas. Chuto shook his head. "No. No, only the burden-bearers," he called. "Our work is to breed and to train. These are no ordinary llamas, boy, that can be turned freely into the world outside. These belong to—" Chuto stopped, a look of dismay clouding his serene and peaceful face. He stood looking at the boy, greatly troubled at what he had almost said. He gestured toward the flock. He could not speak.

For once Cusi's affection for the old man was stronger than his curiosity. He turned without a word and continued his selection. But something had gone from the day. This was a task now. The joy of its being an adventure was gone. Cusi knew that the llamas were to be given to the family living in the lower valley. He had dared to dream that perhaps Chuto would take him along when he went to give the gifts. Now he knew he would not be asked to go. A fire of resentment kindled within him.

When the last llama had been selected and there were twelve proud beasts standing together, Cusi could endure being silent no longer. He asked, "You will go now?"

Chuto's voice when he replied was as quiet and serene as ever, for he had recovered from his recent dismay. Now he said, "Yes," in answer to Cusi's question.

Cusi took heart and ventured another question. "To the lower valley?" he asked.

Chuto again answered, "Yes," and added, "It is where I always take them."

Cusi forgot his resentment in surprise. "Why, I saw this family move in. I saw them clear a place for their shelter. I saw them build it. They could not have been there last year."

Chuto said, "There were other families there in other years."

Cusi was more surprised than ever. "But I never saw them. These were the first I saw."

Chuto laughed. "Did you look?" he asked teasingly, and at Cusi's headshake he said, "Young birds look down from the nest only when they are nearly ready to fly."

There was something in the old man's words that held a promise for the boy. Could the old man mean that some day he, Cusi, would know the answers to his troubled questions? The boy felt a sudden flight of hope.

Chuto went to sit by the corral wall. He went to sit, to think, and silently to pray. Cusi gazed after him. He knew that the

Indian was deep in prayer. He knew it by the look in the old man's eyes, open but unseeing. He knew it by the look on the old man's face, closed to the world around him. He knew it by the look of the old man's hands, at rest and still.

Suddenly the boy could not bear to watch Chuto talking with his gods. It was like looking at something that was not for one to see.

Nor could the boy wait until the man finished praying, wait to watch him go down the trail on an unshared mission.

Cusi turned away.

11. THE SIGN

As the young boy turned away, he looked at once for Misti. As usual Suncca, the dog, was crouched nearby, watching his master's movements. But where was Misti? Misti also was always close, proud and arrogant, but loving and waiting. Where was Misti? Cusi looked again. Then he saw the llama.

Misti was standing in the distance at the edge of the ychugrass meadow. He was watching Cusi. When he saw the boy looking toward him the black llama walked away, then turned to look again. Cusi was mystified. Wanting to see what the llama would do, the boy walked toward him a few steps then stopped. Again and again Misti would walk away, stopping to turn, to look at the boy, to coax him forward.

"That black one!" Cusi whispered. "That black one! He wants me to follow him." Then he called, "Wait for me, Misti! I'm coming."

Misti understood. He waited quietly until Cusi was almost with him. Then he turned and walked swiftly away.

Cusi followed. They were now in the thicket of twisted trees that separated the meadow from the rising mountain slope. There were many trails through the thicket, mostly those used by small mountain animals coming to the meadow stream to drink. For a time this one meandered along, joining other trails or winding back in lazy fashion. Cusi was amused. Misti must be playing some kind of game with him.

Then the trail turned abruptly. Almost immediately they entered a steep-walled narrow canyon. At first the walls were of natural rock, but farther on Cusi noticed that they had been built of stone. So cleverly had man's work matched nature's that Cusi had to retrace his steps and touch with fingertips the line that separated rugged rock from smooth-cut stone. At almost the same place on the opposite wall the stone began. Cusi was interested, but Misti was impatient. His tasseled ears bobbed in annoyance. Cusi laughed, and his laughter sounded hollow and unreal. At the sound he too was seized with a desire to hurry. He was not now following the llama in an idle, playful mood. He had caught the animal's impatience and insistence.

The canyon hallway narrowed to a flight of hand-hewn steps, going down, going down, going down as far as the boy could see. The way was so narrow now that Misti would have difficulty in turning around if they should have need to turn.

The walls were moss-covered and damp and cold and clammy smelling. The sunlight did not reach the crevice trail, and the steps were blotted in purple shadow. There was the sound of water dripping. Drip, drip, it dropped upon stone. Cusi could see no break in the stones of either walls or steps. He could see no trickle dripping, feel no splash as it fell drop by drop against the stone. But he could hear it, each sound distinct and slow and by itself.

Misti was a black shape before him in the softer shadows. Step by step by step by step, the llama and the boy went down the cold stone steps.

Then the stairway ended. Cusi gasped. Directly in front of him was a flat clifflike rock covered with ferns and purple orchids. The air was heavy and sickish sweet with the odor of a tall, bell-shaped flower that grew in tangled beauty against the cliff rock.

At the opposite side of the stage-like canyon there were fallen walls of a ruined temple of pearl-white granite. Beneath the walls was a massive carved stone seat. Cusi walked nearer, Misti watching him.

Then it seemed that the purple shadows lifted and the small canyon was filled with silvery light. Cusi rubbed his eyes and opened them again. Perhaps it just seemed lighter now that he was accustomed to the darkness. The explanation comforted him. Everything was real and everyday. He had by accident stumbled on a new trail.

His mountain world was full of trails and full of ancient ruins. Temples to the Moon and the Stars, the Thunder and Lightning and Rain, were in every valley and on every precipice.

Then he looked behind the carved throne. On a raised stone platform was a white boulder, body-length in thickness but higher than he could see. Along its edges were large, smooth-drilled holes. Cusi's whole body was still with awe and reverence. Without being told, he knew what the rock had been used for.

In the days of the Old when the proud Inca ruled the land the tribal priests had tied the Sun on his way through the heavens. They had tied him to a snow-white boulder with ropes of gold. It was at the winter solstice that they tied the Sun there so he would not go away and leave the world in cold and darkness.

Cusi looked up at the stone dais on which the great Sun had rested. He looked again. He walked nearer to see better.

The black llama watched him with eyes that were ancient and wise and sad with the grief of a conquered people.

On the carved stone lay a pair of golden sandals. Cusi knelt to see them. They were small, too small for him to wear. They were delicate and lovely. They were perfect, as if they had been left there yesterday. Should he touch them? Could he handle them? Dare he take them to have and to keep and to treasure for always?

Then Cusi heard the Amauta's words as clearly as he had heard them that day before the Wise Man left him. "Your heart is good and brave. It is yours to command your actions."

Cusi touched the sandals. He picked them up. He held them tenderly in his thin young hands. When he had feasted his eyes on their shining beauty, he wrapped them in the folds of his poncho.

They were his. In some way that he did not know, they had always belonged to him. They were his. His heart told him they were his.

Far above him he heard Misti's hoofs tapping, tapping, as he climbed the steep stone stairway.

Cusi did not remember following the llama. He did not remember walking the homeward trail. He knew only that at last he was there. He saw the fire of llama dung before the shelter door. Then he realized it was night. The stars hung low. A pale moon spilled silver light across a cold blue highland valley.

The boy stumbled toward the fire. Then he saw Chuto sitting there. Chuto looked tired. He looked worn. He looked old and troubled. He sat there hunched in his poncho, chewing coca leaves to give him strength for waiting.

Now he looked up at the dark, vividly handsome boy standing before him. At once he knew that whatever had happened was wonderful and good. He waited for the boy to speak.

Cusi said in unbelief, "It is night."

The Indian answered, "Yes. It is almost dawn."

There was silence. Fire smoke curled upward in a blue line. Misti walked among the other llamas. At once, night silence was broken by the little noises of dawn. Birds chirped in the thicket. The llamas began humming, humming softly like the background of whispered music for a song.

Chuto spoke again. "I went and I returned. Then I waited for your returning."

"Yes," Cusi whispered. "Yes, you waited for me." He knelt on the ground by the Old One's side. Softly he told of all that had happened. Slowly he unfolded the sandals and held them to the light of the fire flames.

"Ah—h," Chuto said in quiet happiness. "It is a sign, my Cusi. It is a sign."

The old Indian went into the hut. Cusi sat looking at the golden sandals and letting happiness overflow in his heart like waters overflowing their rocky basin in a spraying waterfall.

Chuto came out of the hut with his medicine bag. He busied himself before the fire, making a mixture of coca leaves and llama fat. This he burned in the fire and watched the volume and the shape and the direction of the smoke it made. He did this four times. At last he was satisfied.

He spoke to Cusi or to himself, the boy was not certain which, but he listened. Chuto said, "It is the sign I have been waiting for. There is something he wants, something he needs to find. He will find it." He was quiet for a while, looking at the fire; then he turned, saying, "Tomorrow you will go alone to Cuzco, the Holy City. Somewhere along the way you will find what you desire."

Cusi knew what it was that he wanted to find. He would have liked to say to Chuto, "I want to find a family. I want to know the joy of having mother and father, sisters and brothers." He could not say it. He would have liked to say, "I need not go as far as Cuzco. What I want is in the valley below us. I have seen it." But he could not say it.

The fire flames flickered. They blazed anew. Chuto rose. He was not dreaming now. He was quick and brisk and efficient. Pointing to the eastern sky, he said, "We have just time enough to make the Sunrise Call. Then you must be on your way." With his lips he gestured to the stone corral. "They are loaded and waiting."

Cusi looked. There were seven llamas loaded with wool. They were standing quietly, chewing their cuds. "How did you know?" Cusi asked. The Old One laughed softly. "My heart told me that on this day you would receive the sign and that you would leave me."

For a second Cusi did not want to go; then he looked at the golden sandals and knew that he must follow the sign. He did not ask himself whether he would return. He had no need for asking, because he knew the answer. He would find a family. Chuto had said so, and Chuto had never failed him.

Once more he folded the precious sandals in his poncho and followed Chuto down the sunrise trail.

12. THE VALLEY BELOW

At last. At last. Cusi was going down the llama trail. He was going searching for a family.

Black Misti, proud and beautiful, was at his elbow. Behind him, marching in single file, were seven yellow-brown llamas as proud and as beautiful as Misti. They marched in perfect order; each pointed little hoof was placed with delicate exactness on the slippery rocks of the steep, narrow trail. The red tassels in their ears kept time to the tinkle, tinkle of the lead llama's bell. Their rounded loads of wool piled high on their backs bobbed in rhythm to their marching feet.

Cusi's bright blue poncho swung backward as he stepped along at the head of the llama line. His coca bag tied at one side of his sash and the bag of parched corn at the other swished gaily against his knees. Around his neck on a slender cord was his medicine bag. In it in neat, tidy bundles were a pinch of salt, a pinch of dried herbs, and an ancient knife. There was also powdered tobacco in the bag—powdered tobocco for snake bite in case Cusi or his llamas met an unfriendly snake on the mountain trail. The medicine bag swung from side to side. The woolen tassel on the boy's long pointed cap nodded. In fact everything moved with the moving procession.

Everything moved except the golden sandals. Wrapped in

a square of vicuña cloth, they lay close and safe against the young boy's heart.

It was a beautiful morning, a morning bright with promise and shining with hope.

Cusi and his llamas walked happily down the llama trail. No cloud marred the blue sky. No wind cried in the canyons. The new day waited breathless and beautiful for Cusi to walk through it from its blue dawning until its purple dusk.

The boy and the llamas walked down the mountain trail. Above them in Hidden Valley, Chuto was left to mourn their going. Below them lay the lower valley, lost to view now because of the bulging mountain. But it lay there at the foot of the trail. By midday when the Great Sun paused to let the shadows rest, Cusi would have reached the clearing. He would be standing before the shelter door of the family he felt he knew so well.

But even in his eagerness to reach his journey's desire, the boy did not forget that first and last and always he had llamas to shepherd. He let them wander frequently in the little side canyons where the ychu grass grew to feed them. "You will not graze at night, my llamas," he told them with affection, "so now I give you time to eat the rich grass you need to give you strength."

After the llamas had eaten, they folded their legs beneath them to rest. Their rounded loads looked like grass huts, squatting low on the ychu grass. Cusi laughed aloud to see them. At his laughter the llamas began to hum in llama pleasure to let the whole world know that all was well. Cusi hummed with them; then he leaped to his feet, giving the llama call, "Come, llamas. Come, llamas." As always the animals obeyed him at once and began their stately march again.

Cusi munched parched corn as he took his place at the head of the procession. He said to Misti in a teasing tone, "I am not as proud as you. I do not mind if I must eat as I walk along."

They went down, down the llama trail and came closer and closer to the lower valley. Cusi began recognizing landmarks he had spotted from his lookout rock in the valley above. He saw the burned tree that lightning had struck, standing black and bold, a lone sentinel. He crossed the trickling stream that bubbled along to join the mighty river. Everything was hot and still. The shadows had folded themselves beneath the trees and the shrubbery. The Great Sun was in mid-sky, looking down on the boy and on the llamas.

Cusi stopped. He was almost there. Sweat dampened his forehead at the edge of his knitted cap and ran in little rivers down his brown cheeks. The palms of his hands were wet; he wiped them on his white trouser legs. He was here at last, in the valley below. He was where his dreams had led him. Only a few more steps now, and he would stand at the far end of the clearing. Then he and his llamas would walk across it. He knew every step of the way from having watched it so often. They would walk across the clearing and stand before the shelter door. Someone would answer his shout of greeting. The father, or the children perhaps, or the mother? All of them? Yes, that would be the way it would happen. They would all come crowding to the door, laughing and talking and welcoming him. Would he say, "I want to be a part of your family," or would they know it, Cusi wondered. Would it be a difficult thing to say? Would he be brave enough and bold enough?

Cusi looked up the mountain, trying to find the valley that lay hiding just beneath the line of eternal snow. Chuto was there. Chuto the good one, the kind one, the Old One, who loved him and had taught him all he knew. What was Chuto doing now? Cusi wondered. Was he sitting by the fire, thinking? Was he sitting by the corral wall deep in prayer? Was he crouched on the overhanging rock, watching the boy he had told good-by? That was what he was doing! Suddenly Cusi knew it. He could see Chuto on the rock as plainly as he had seen him every day of his life. He could feel the old man's thoughts giving him courage. He could feel the old man's love giving him strength to do that which his heart had bidden.

Cusi turned around. He swung his poncho folds over his shoulder. He felt the sandal bundle close to his panting heart. He walked across the clearing, and the black llama and the seven yellow-brown llamas followed him in stately single file.

Cusi walked across the clearing and the llamas followed. They walked across the clearing to where the shelter should have been.

There was no shelter. The ground was bare and trampled by the feet of men, of children, and of llamas, but there was not a sign of the shelter that had stood there. Ashes of the cooking fire, yes, but ashes dead and cold. Cusi was stunned. Perhaps the shelter had burned? But no. There was no charred wood. There was no burned thatch. There was nothing but footmarks on the trampled ground.

Cusi never knew how long he stood there. Long enough to grow older. Long enough to see dreams die.

The llamas waited expectantly, their sad, dark eyes on the boy they knew as master. Misti nudged him. The Great Sun moved through the heavens on his way to put the day to bed. The shadows stole out from their resting place and, strengthened by their brief siesta, grew longer with the lengthening day. An old man on the mountaintop let his tears drop to heal the heartache of a lonely boy.

Cusi knew it. He had been so close to Chuto, so near him, so much a part of his world, that he knew when the Old One cried. He could sense the Old One's tears. He knew that they were dropping to cool the burning of his heart, to soothe his aching disappointment, to wash all his bitterness away.

He did not ask why, why, why—why were they gone? Why could they not have been there to take him in? Why had Chuto let him come, knowing that all was gone? Cusi was learning to accept the way that had been laid out before him. He was learning not to wonder, not to question, not to rebel, but to go forth step by step and step by step as the trail became deeper and the signs along the way more clearly marked.

He had one thought to cling to. Both Chuto and the Amauta had told him, "Follow your heart." Even the minstrel had said it, not in the same words, perhaps, but meaning the same.

"Follow your heart." Cusi knew where that would lead him. It would lead him to the haven of family love and family security.

Misti nudged the boy again. Cusi looked at him through a mist of unshed tears. He looked at his llama and tried to smile. "All right, Misti," he told the proud, black llama. "All right. We will go to Cuzco. I think that you and Chuto knew that was what would happen."

The young boy led his llamas back across the clearing to the trail again. When he had reached its shadowed coolness, he sat awhile to rest his head upon his knees.

The llamas waited—not grazing, not resting, not humming. This was not the time. This was not the place. This was only waiting for their young master to take heart again.

By and by Cusi sighed. He raised his head. He rose and gave the llama call. "Come, llamas. Come, llamas." The llamas obeyed him. Arrogantly they walked behind him.

Soon the mountain world of Hidden Valley and the valley below it was left behind. No one paused. No one hesitated. No one stopped. No one looked back.

The boy and his llamas marched on. Lower Valley was behind them now.

+ suspense (pull up)
+ entertain -

13. CUZCO TRAIL

The trail grew steeper. Cusi and his llamas were climbing again. Mountain peaks piled upon mountain peaks. They rolled and swelled and piled higher and yet higher. They encircled the world. They towered above the world. They enclosed the world within itself. Only a brown ribbon of trail wound in and out and around them. Only a boy and his llamas moved along the winding trail.

From time to time the llamas stopped to graze, but they would not rest. Cusi scolded, "You are tired, my llamas. You need to rest."

The llamas walked on. If Cusi faltered, Misti nudged him. If Cusi stumbled, Misti poked him. The lead llama's bell had an urgent tinkle. "Hurry. Hurry. Hurry," it seemed to say. "Hurry. Hurry. Hurry."

Shadows blurred in the evening's light. The mountains misted as night stole into the highlands. The trail darkened. Cusi began hunting a side canyon where he could bed his llamas for the night.

Then he noticed a fork in the trail. This surprised him, for highland trails have but one goal as a usual thing. The side trail was poorly marked and evidently little used. Cusi stood looking at it, wondering if perhaps it led to the side canyon that he had been looking for. Should he take it, he wondered, or should he keep his small flock on the well-marked, deeper, clearer trail? While he was thinking about which way to take, Misti crowded against him, pushing forward on the smaller trail. Then he stopped to look back at his young master. Cusi laughed, remembering the other time that Misti had led instead of following. It was the first time the boy had laughed since midday in Lower Valley. The llamas liked it. They crowded forward, pushing Cusi along. "All right. All right!" Cusi laughed at them. "Come, llamas. Come, llamas, this is our way."

Almost at once the way became clear and deep. Then it was paved with cobblestones. Cusi was surprised. He knew he was not near enough to Cuzco to have a paved trail. This was something new. He was surprised but he was not afraid. He followed Misti, who was still in the lead. The other seven followed him closely.

Then, rounding a curve, he saw a dull, light haze—not the flickering flame of a tiny cooking fire. This must be the merged light of many cooking fires.

The boy was tired, but he made his steps come faster and longer. The llamas also were hurrying, and the lead bell sang out, "Hurry-hurry-hurry," tinkling so fast the sounds ran into each other, making one tinkle sound.

They reached a gate in a high stone wall. A guard, an Indian, stood before the huge gate. He said, in Cusi's own tongue, "You are expected. Enter"

Other Indians appeared, stealing forward like shadows from the darker shadows of the high walls. They led the llamas away, to unload them, to feed them, to bed them for the night.

A younger Indian, almost Cusi's age, beckoned the boy along the narrow streets that were lined with stone, high and cold and gray-white in the new night's deepening darkness. Along the narrow streets they went, walking swiftly, walking silently in a still and ghostlike world. At last they came to three stone towers separated by walled courtyards and stone archways. They passed two of the towers, then turned and climbed a flight of steps to the third tower, standing majestic and grand against the night.

The young Indian led Cusi to a great arched door. Slowly it swung open and a voice asked, "Is he here?"

The young Indian answered, "He is here."

Cusi walked through the doorway and stood in a high-ceilinged room. Its walls were of white stone and perfectly bare. Nothing hung against their cold white marble. At one end of the room was a carved stone seat exactly like the stone that Cusi had seen the day he found the sandals. He looked around, almost expecting to see delicate golden sandals standing side by side at the foot of the throne. There was nothing there. Quietly he felt the bundle wrapped in vicuña cloth close to his heart. They were there, safe, where he had put them.

By the high stone seat there was a table made of stone and a stone block beside it. Cusi looked around. He was alone. The Indian guide had disappeared. Then the boy saw an old man approaching.

The Old One looked so much like Chuto that Cusi gasped and would have run to him, but he sensed that it was not Chuto. The Old One wore the fringed turban and the golden earplugs. He did not speak, but motioned Cusi to sit on the stone block by the table.

A woman entered, stately and beautiful, with the peace of living days enriching her still, brown face. Cusi could never remember how she was dressed, but he remembered, or thought he remembered, that on her feet were golden sandals like the ones he had found and was keeping close to his heart.

The woman asked, "Is he here?"

The Old One answered, "He is here."

The woman brought food to Cusi, guinea pig and sweet potatoes, fish from the sea and figs from the coastlands. In a low voice like the minstrel's Pipes of Pan she said, "Eat, my Son."

Cusi was hungry. He was tired and bewildered, but he was hungry. He was amazed and filled with wonder, but he was hungry. He ate the food set before him. It tasted good.

No word was spoken until Cusi had finished eating. Then the Old One said, "He is well; you have seen him. Is it enough?"

The woman nodded and smiled. "It is enough," she said and she was gone. As quietly, as quickly as she had come, she left. The room seemed empty.

The Old One spoke again. "They told me you were coming."

Cusi felt no need to ask, "Who told you?" He knew. Instead he asked, "The family came here?" The Indian answered, "They passed by here, leading the llamas Chuto gave them. Last year, this year, next year, they always pass by. These families and their gift llamas are the cord that ties our past to our future that we may never end."

Cusi thought about this answer for a while. It made sense and it did not make sense. It answered his question and it did not answer it. He tried another. "What is this place?"

"It is an Ayllu, which means a town of the Ancient People. We were here in the beginning when the Inca ruled the world." Cusi was about to ask another question when the old man, surprisingly, answered it before it was asked. "I am the Year Father of the Ayllu," he said. "I care for the People. I touch the past and hold it for the future. I know you whom they call Cusi, and I know also the one called Chuto who has guided and cared for you. I know what you do and why it has been so ordered. You too will know these things when your hand has drawn the curtain that hides them. Go your way and weep not that it circles."

Cusi jumped to his feet. He was not awed now or confused. He pleaded, and the desperate need of an answer to his plea freed him of any fear that he might have had. "How can I know when my hand has drawn the curtain? How can I know? How can I know?"

But the Old One shook his head. "You are part of a pattern," he said. "Follow your heart. May the Inca's blessing go with you."

The young Indian appeared at Cusi's shoulder. "Come," he told the boy. He led Cusi along the hallway to the great arched door. He led Cusi along the silent, narrow streets. What was this place? Were the people here living people or were they walking in the past? Cusi shivered.

The Indian touched his arm. "We have reached the llama corral. Sleep well in the place that belongs to you, here among your llamas. At the Sunrise Call the gates will be opened for your departing." Then he faded away, a shadowed part of a darker, bigger shadow.

Cusi curled up beside Misti, where he had slept as long as he could remember sleeping. He whispered sleepily to his pet, "I must think about these things that have happened. It will help pass this night away." With these words his eyes closed. The tired boy slept, slept without thinking, slept without dreaming, slept without moving the whole night through.

He was wakened by the familiar words of the Sunrise Call. Someone was chanting:

"O Sun! Great Father of the Inca . . ."

And the people of the Ayllu answered:

"Who has gone before us."

The chanter called:

"Great Father of the children of the Inca . . ."

And again the people answered, saying:

"Who remain in this thy world."

This was the call that Chuto made each dawn to the Sun's coming. This was the Sunrise Call he had taught Cusi. Now Cusi answered with the people of the Ayllu. They said:

". . . is now but a shadow
in the memory of man."

They said:

". . . is as the dust of the earth
blown before a willful wind."

They said:

"O Sun! O Sun!
Great Father of the Inca."

As the last words of the Call sounded forth into the dawn sky of morning, the young Indian guide was again at Cusi's side. "It is time that you go," he said softly.

Cusi wanted to say, "I do not want to go." He wanted to say, "I need to see more. I need to understand more. I need to stay."

But he did not say these things. He said nothing. He followed the guide to the great gate in the wide wall. There were his llamas waiting for him. Cusi heard himself saying, "Take these to the Esteemed Old One. Take these to the Mother One who gave me food." Cusi counted out five of his flock, five yellow-brown llamas with their packs of wool. Among them was the lead llama. The others would need his bell now that they would not hear the voice of their master again. Cusi felt no surprise at what he was saying or what he was doing. It felt right to do this thing. It was what Chuto would have done.

The guide turned the llamas from the gate. He turned them back to the city. He said, "The blood of nobility runs rich and true." Then he opened the Ayllu gate. The boy and his three llamas went through it. They heard the clang as it shut behind them. They heard the rasp of the stone bolt being drawn into its place. They went back over the trail to the fork.

Cusi heard the tinkle of a llama bell. As he turned he saw that Misti wore a golden bell on his night-black throat. Had they known what he would do, he wondered.

At the fork Cusi did not hesitate. He took the well-marked trail. He took the cared-for one. He took the well-trod one. This was the trail to Cuzco. He knew it.

Nothing happened. The sun rode in the heavens. The wind cried in the canyons. The llamas walked and rested and grazed and hummed and walked again. Cusi ate parched corn. He chewed a coca leaf to keep his strength within him.

At midday they reached the Cuzco road. They passed through the pueblo of San Sebastián. They passed through the pueblo of Santo Domingo. No one stopped them. No one spoke to them. No one noticed them. It was only a boy and his llamas. It was only a highland shepherd. No one cared.

By evening time they had reached the hills of Cuzco. Cusi stood on a hilltop, looking down into the town. There was the Temple of the Sun. There was the Temple of the Moon. There was the Temple of the Maidens of the Sun. They were as the Amauta had described them.

Cusi knew that beneath the ancient paving stones of the city's streets ran the three sacred rivers of Cuzco. He knew that from the hilltop where he stood ancient secret tunnels wound their way into the heart of the city. He knew these things because the Amauta had taught them to him.

He saw people crowding the narrow, crooked streets. He saw them climbing the old, old stairways. He did not know them. They were strange.

He heard the evening church bells ringing in the tower of Santo Domingo Church. The sky behind the church was crimson and gold from the setting sun. White pigeons flew in and out of the church-tower windows. The bells kept ringing. It was the Angelus, blessing the people with evening prayer. But this was new and unknown to Cusi. The Amauta had not told him of temples built to a different god. Cusi saw brown-robed priests going into the church. Even from where he stood he could see they were not Indian. They were strangers.

Cusi looked backward, but all he saw were the deep, sad eyes of his llamas, questioning him. He turned again to the strange town at the foot of the hill. He began to climb down the steep steps leading to the city wall. Close behind him came the llamas,their rounded loads of wool bobbing, bobbing as the steep steps were descended.

The boy and his small herd reached the city walls, but they did not enter. A Spanish guardsman would not let them enter. He said sternly to the highland shepherd, "Has no one told you, boy, that llamas cannot stay overnight in the city, within these walls?"

Cusi was angered. "Llamas not allowed in the Holy Place of the Inca?" he asked. "Llamas belong here, as I belong."

The guardsman laughed. An Indian appeared from the walled gate and spoke kindly to the highland boy. "I have been expecting you," he said quietly, ignoring the Spaniard beside him. "Spend the night here with your llamas. Tomorrow I will take your herd and you into the city."

Once again Cusi curled up among his llamas to spend a night in a strange place. This night he dreamed. He dreamed of the sandals he carried in the folds of his poncho. He dreamed of the woman who served him food in the Ayllu and called him "son." His dream was vague and mixed up and unreal but it carried a message. The young boy could not understand the message; not yet. But he could hold it in his heart to make him brave.

The lights of Cuzco were bright. The stars hung low, and the moon smiled down on the Holy Place of the Ancients.

Outside the city wall a herd boy slept and dreamed a dream he could not understand.

14. THE MARKETPLACE

"Open your eyes. Open your heart to this day that is waiting for you." Cusi moved, but his eyes were so heavy with sleep he could not open them. The singsong voice repeated, "Open your eyes. Open your heart. Open your mind to this day."

Cusi sat up, rubbing sleep from his eyes and dreams from his mind. Who was this Indian who kept telling him to waken? Where was he? He looked around at high, bare hills and high stone walls. What was this place? Who was this stranger looking so intently at him?

Then he remembered! This was Cuzco! This was his city! This was the day he had waited for so long. He looked at the Indian, who was repeating, "Open your eyes. Open your heart. Open your mind. The day is waiting." Cusi flashed him a remembering smile. This was the Indian who had befriended him the night before.

The boy jumped to his feet, eager to meet what lay waiting for him. He looked toward the eastern sky and saw the first rosy hint of dawn. Knowing that no Indian begins his day until the Sun comes and he pays homage, Cusi turned to his new friend, expecting to follow him to the holy place held sacred to this duty. He was surprised that the man made no move to depart. The Indian was still standing by Cusi and his llamas. Then the boy saw that the man was looking toward the east and that his face was stilled in prayer although no words came forth welcoming the glory of day. His arms were folded beneath his poncho, not raised in salute. To one not knowing, he would seem just an Indian standing quietly in the cold gray of a mountain dawn.

Cusi sensed that the Sunrise Call was being spoken deep in the heart of the man beside him. The boy did as the man was doing. He folded his arms beneath his poncho. He stood silent and relaxed and turned his eyes to the dawning day. Within his heart the Sunrise Call came whispering, came soaring on the wings of feeling, lifting heavenward without the need of sound.

Day burst in mighty majesty through the night-curtained sky. The Sun came and blessed Cuzco.

The Indian spoke, now that the Sun had come. He said, "The rivers of Cuzco lie hidden beneath the cobblestones of its streets. Likewise the ways of our Ancients flow in steady streams beneath the surface of our days."

Cusi was beginning to recognize thoughts that men had, although they might be spoken with strange words. He understood now what the man was telling him and with this new understanding came a new happiness and a new feeling of ease and security. He replied, "Covered water cannot be muddied," and the man answered, "Nor its course changed."

As they spoke, they walked by the guardsman at the gate. It was the same guardsman who had spoken so sharply to the boy the night before. Now he looked at the man and boy and llamas indifferently. He had noticed the Indian waiting at the gate so patiently for several days. He has been waiting for the boy, he thought to himself. Some relative, perhaps. Well, it was a good thing the highland boy had someone who would show him what to do. Imagine! Thinking he could come into Cuzco with his llamas at night! The guardsman laughed. "These Indians," he muttered, "haven't a notion of what laws are or how to keep them." He laughed again as memory of the mountain boy's fiery answer came back to him. "Llamas belong here as I belong!" the boy had said. Good thing he could speak their Indian language, the guardsman thought comfortably. Gave him a chance to know what they were thinking. Imagine! Thinking he and his llamas had a right to Cuzco! Doesn't know they've been conquered for four hundred years, he thought. He kept on thinking about the Indians and their llamas.

But the man and the boy he was thinking about never gave a thought to him. They were thinking about Cuzco. Their Cuzco, beloved and sacred and old! They were walking in their Holy City. They were walking along the old, worn ways of their golden past. It was not the way of a dead or conquered people. It was the way of the Inca, and the Inca had never died.

Cusi was talking eagerly, pointing to places, asking questions, saying happily, "Oh, yes, yes. That is the way the Amauta said it would be."

The man, the boy, the llamas, walked single file along the Street of the Stone of the Twelve Angles. The Indian pointed out the intricate stone cutting proudly. An immense, thick, high, heavy stone had been cut with such patience, had been fitted with such exactness into the stones around it that it seemed as if a divine and not a human hand had placed it there.

They passed by the high, rounded tower of the Temple of the Sun Maidens. The new Sun glistening on the damp, moss-covered walls made teardrops shimmer in the light of the young new day.

They walked through the narrow, dark passageway of the Street of the Seven Snakes. The Indian silently pointed out the seven carved serpents of stone. He did not say what they meant or why they were there. The boy knew as the man knew, as Indians know.

The rivers of Cuzco flowed unheard, unseen, unhampered, beneath the cobblestones of the streets.

At last the travelers reached a flight of broad stone steps winding downward to the central plaza. Misti's golden bell made a sweet tinkle as the black llama followed his master with arrogance and with pride. The two yellow-brown llamas followed Misti in dignified, measured single file.

They came to the plaza of the city.

Cusi had never seen anything like it before. In the square that was formed by the tall buildings around it was grass, a softer, greener, thicker grass than the ychu of the highland valleys. In a bright border around the grass flowers were growing—not fragile, hiding, little mountain flowers, but big, bold flowers in bold colors, like a rainbow resting on the ground.

The buildings were strange too. They were flower shades in color with red tile roofs. There were windows of glass that could be seen through like rain mist in morning. There were great doors to be closed like gates in the city walls.

And people! Indians, Latins, those of the two-blood mixture. There were others, stranger than the mixed bloods—Arab, Anglo-Saxon, Chinese. Each kind was as strange, as vivid, as arresting as the flowers in the plaza.

Cusi would have liked to stay here in the plaza, feasting his eyes and his mind on the sights he saw, but the Indian beckoned him onward. "Llamas are not allowed to rest within the city. They must keep walking," he said simply.

Cusi called softly, "Come, my llamas. Come, my llamas. We are not wanted here." Misti tinkled his bell in answer, and the animals kept on, not hurrying, not hesitating, but marching along in precise, sedate, indifferent dignity.

They passed the church that Cusi had seen from the hilltop the evening before. White doves still flew in and out of the bell tower. The bell still rang its slow, toned prayer. The doors were open. Cusi could see candle lights and kneeling people.

But there was no time for stopping. The Indians went on. The llamas went on. Reluctantly Cusi followed along a winding street lined on either side with candle shops. There were candles of every size, of every color, for every day in the year and for every need and for every dream. There were candles to be burned to bring the burner love and luck and happiness and health. There were black candles to be burned for evil power. Cusi did not loiter here. There was magic in the candle shops. The boy felt safer when he and the llamas followed the Indian guide and turned from the strange narrow way to enter the marketplace.

There the Indian left him, saying merely, "I leave you for now. When you have traded the wool your llamas carry, I will come for them. Have no fear. There are those to serve you. The Inca takes care of his own." As he finished speaking, he disappeared in the crowd of people swarming through the market.

Cusi and his llamas were left alone. They were alone in a crowd of people. Cusi felt more alone than he had felt ever before among lofty mountain peaks or along the empty highland trails.

Gradually his loneliness wore away amid the movements, the colors, and the sounds of the market. Gradually the shepherd boy and his llamas began to mingle with the people and to enjoy the business, the excitement, the gaiety around them.

Close by were the food venders. Each group had its own kind of food, its own place in the market, and its own cotton cloth shade tied across bamboo poles. Children sat patiently by their family food stores. Babies and dogs slept soundly and peacefully by hills of marble-size potatoes, mounds of pearly Spanish onions, piles of little scarlet tomatoes, bunches of bright orange carrots, bundles of dried coca leaves, and stacks of green corn ears, beanstalks, and sugar cane.

"Buy an egg, boy," a smiling woman told him. "I will trade you an egg for a llama load of wool. That's a good bargain." Everyone laughed. Cusi laughed also. He was too shy to talk, but laughter came easily.

He stood before the sugar cane. Sugar cane was new to him. At first he refused the short round stalk the man held out to him. Finally curiosity overcame shyness, and he accepted the gift, sucking in the sweet juice where it ran from the cut the man made. It tasted good. It tasted wonderful. Cusi began to barter. "A handful of wool for two handfuls of cane stalks," he ventured.

The man came to life immediately. He loved to trade. All Indians love to trade. Offers flew back and forth. The sugar-cane man and Cusi were enjoying themselves. Before long the trade was completed to both their and the onlookers' satisfaction. Cusi began to unload some wool from the woven net bag on Misti's back. Then the man demanded yapa. Since this was Cusi's first experience in trading, he did not know what yapa was. Yapa is the little more that each side in a trade must give as proof of good will. The trading began over again as to how much yapa one should give and how much yapa one should receive. When the bartering was finished at last, Cusi loaded an armful of sugar cane on top of the remaining wool on Misti's back. He went on, happy with the sweet taste of sugar cane and happy with the sweet taste of barter.

He did not feel timid now, or shy. He felt like a seasoned trader and he swaggered a bit as he led his llamas to the potato vender to trade wool for potatoes and yapa. He must not forget yapa. It was an important part of trading.

It was noontime before the two yellow-brown llamas had exchanged their loads of wool for potatoes, for green corn, for dried beanstalks and dried coca leaves and lumps of lime. Only Misti's wool load remained, except for the bit of wool that had gone in payment for the sugar cane.

What to trade Misti's wool for, that was the problem. For a long time the boy stood before the trinket vender. Spread out in tempting array were pink and purple plastic combs, little round mirrors with pictures of waterfalls on their tin backs, beads of every size and hue, big and little buttons more color-ful than any rainbow, pictures of saints, cards of safety pins. They were wonderful things, but how could he use them? He needed neither buttons nor safety pins. The mirrors were magic and therefore not good to possess. No, these things, although desirable and beautiful, were not for him. With a sigh the boy passed on.

His next stop was before the display of dyes, roots and herbs and minerals, but he did not stay long. The drab powdered dye materials held no hint of the colors they would produce. They did not lure him with the secret of their colors.

On the steps of the Indoor Market the medicine men dis-played their wares. In neatly woven bags the drugs were shown to the passer-by to tempt him whether he was sick or well. After long hesitation and longer bargaining Cusi traded some more of Misti's load for a dried starfish brought up from the sea. What its curing power was, only the Medicine man and he knew.

Cusi stood on the steps and looked into the dark mysteries of the inside of the huge cavelike building. Near the door were the leather goods, sandals and shoes, saddles and saddlebags. The boy looked beyond these to the knitted sweater and cap section. Finally making up his mind, he spoke softly to his llamas to follow him and went inside. Instantly he was stopped. Llamas could not come inside, they told him. Cusi turned back. He could not leave his llamas untended.

The Indian guide of the morning was at his side. "I will watch them for you," he said. Cusi was surprised. Where had the man come from, he wondered. But since he was there, why not let him help? The boy smiled his acceptance of the offer and went inside.

He bartered for sweaters and for cotton trousers, one size to fit him and one size larger. He examined the knitted caps— red for the young and white for the old. He fingered them and examined them. He set two aside, one red and one white.

When he went outside to get Misti's wool load to pay for his purchases he was not surprised to find the man and the llamas waiting for him. He knew neither robbery nor theft and therefore did not fear them.

The man made no comment about the loads. When Cusi had unpacked Misti's wool sack and repacked it with the new possessions, the Indian said, "I'll take them now." Cusi looked his questions. Where would the man take the llamas? What would Misti do? The man seemed to know what was in the boy's mind, because he answered, "I will take them outside the city to await your orders. You now are free to seek your heart's desire."

A flood of remembrance washed over Cusi, leaving him breathless and weak with anticipation. Ah, his heart's desire! He was free now. He was free to go searching in the market-place, in the plaza, in the city streets, for that which he wanted more than anything. He nodded to the man to take the llamas and turned to whisper something in Misti's ear. The proud black llama listened and looked at him, then turned gravely to follow the man outside the city gates.

Cusi watched them go; the Indian, his Misti, and the other two. There were unshed tears in the boy's dark eyes. Misti's lead bell tinkled, tinkled, tinkled. Even when he could no longer be seen among the milling people, the sweet, clear tinkle called to Cusi. "Find a family. Find a family. Find a family," it seemed to say.

Cusi turned. Where would he go to find his family? The answer came to him with the pealing of the church bell. Quickly he walked through the crowd, a highland boy away from his mountain peaks, a shepherd boy without his llamas.

15. THE FAMILY

Cusi sat in the shade of the church wall. Above him the white doves cooed to their young in the bell-tower nests. His heart beat against the golden sandals he carried in his poncho folds. He had put the sugar cane away in his coca bag and was thoughtfully chewing hard, parched corn kernels, his mid-day meal.

The two great doors of the church were open and from its candle-lit, dim interior came the muffled sounds of prayer, came the musky odor of incense. People went in and out, in and out, in and out. Men and women, children and babies, rich and poor, Indian and white, they went into the church to lay their burdens at the feet of their god. They came out again, rested, to take up the work that god had given them. Cusi watched them. Something told him that he would find his family here.

A thin white dog came to share the shade with him, to scratch his fleas and to watch the people. The dog reminded Cusi of Suncca. Softly he spoke to him. "Suncca, Suncca, come here. Come here." The dog did not answer to the name or the words. He sat watching the people.

An open carriage drew up at the church steps and the young man who was driving jumped down from his seat to help the lady within to alight. Cusi's eyes grew blacker and deeper as the lady came tripping daintily up the worn steps.

Her ruffled skirts fluttered in the wind like flower petals. Her dark eyes were full of laughter as they peeked out through the lacy edges of her mantilla. She must be very good, the young boy thought, because she was so beautiful. Perhaps— a small hope whispered in his heart. Perhaps—but no; such a lady would have no need of a mountain boy for brother.

Cusi turned his eyes away lest the lady see loneliness in them.

A beggar inched toward the beauty as she daintily stepped into the church. Cusi looked at the beggar with contempt. The old man's rags were hanging in shreds and gray with filth. The old man's hair was long and tangled and matted, and his shrewd eyes were sharp and keen. He saw Cusi's glance and instantly shuffled toward him, whining the beggar's prayer. Cusi offered him his bag of parched corn, but the beggar re- fused it. He wanted coins not corn. The thin dog growled, and the beggar moved on, nearer to the church door, nearer to those who might pass by with money to give.

Cusi turned his back. His heart felt sick with disgust. Pov- erty he knew, and hunger and cold, but to beg for it—never! Unconsciously the boy reached up to touch a golden earplug. Sign of Royalty, the minstrel had said, but Cusi was not think- ing of what the minstrel had said. He was thinking of his heart's desire. He was thinking of his folk and a hearth fire and family devotion. He was watching the people.

Two round, fat, roly-poly monks waddled past. They looked like two perky brown day-birds approaching a water pool. Their brown robes swished against their sandaled feet. Their eyes were lowered. They fingered the beads of their rosaries hanging from thick white cords at their waists. Their lips were moving as they silently whispered their prayers.

Their shaven heads were round and red and glistening in the bright, hot sunlight. God was their Father and the saints their brothers. They needed no earthly family. They would not want him.

The young boy sighed. Heat haze danced on the hot stones of the pavement and made rippling rainbows before his tired eyes. He was not used to people or to cities. He was used to mountains, remote and cold and still. He leaned his head against the hot wall and wished for midafternoon to come with the comfort of its shadows. What was Misti doing? Did he know why Cusi stayed within the city walls? Cusi touched the golden sandals hidden safe against his heart. They were his omen. They were his sign. He remembered the peace of the mountains, yes; but he remembered too the lonely, endless days there.

Cusi sat up straighter. He was all intent now. An Indian woman had rounded the corner of the church wall. She was coming toward him. Wide purple woolen skirts flared out from tiny brown feet. Her bright alpaca-woven shoulder shawl was pinned with a long pointed silver spoon-pin. Her upturned red embroidered hat framed a slender brown face, beautiful but searching and sad. Memory stirred within the boy. Was this the woman of the Ayllu? Was this the woman who had given him food and called him son? But no. This one was older. This woman was grieving with a grief that would not let her rest. But she looked like the woman of the Ayllu. She looked like the woman he had dreamed about. Perhaps she too was searching for home and loved ones. Perhaps she would want him as her son. What could he say that would make her know? Cusi's heart beat wildly. His throat was dry. No words came.

The woman trotted past him, her feet making pat-pat noises

on the worn stones before the open church door. Then she turned. She had seen him. She stopped in wonder, one hand covering her mouth in the Indian way. An amazed exclamation burst from her lips. "Golden earplugs," she cried, "golden earplugs! You belong. You are one of them."

Cusi stood up. He moved a step closer to the woman. They looked deep into each other's eyes. This one was older than the Ayllu woman but very, very like her.

Finally the woman spoke again. "You are so like Titu," she said and then, shaking her head, she added, "Titu. He was older when he ran away."

The woman began to walk away, but Cusi could not bear to let her go. "I am Cusi," he said quickly, desperately. Anything to have her stay.

"I know," she answered sadly. "I know. You are the one that Titu gave them in his place." She started on again, then half turned, saying over her shoulder, "Once I was the mother chosen. Titu was my son, but he ran away. I search but I never find him. Tell Chuto—" The woman did not finish. Hurriedly she rounded the corner, the way she had come.

Cusi was stunned. Dumbly he stood, making no sound, making no movement, watching her go.

A hand lightly touched his shoulder. Cusi, startled, turned wide black eyes up to the laughing dark ones of the Spanish beauty who had come in a carriage. She had seen him then as she tripped lightheartedly into the church. Could it mean— but Cusi could not think! He still was numbed from his encounter with the Indian woman. He could only wait.

The woman smiled at him and said in Spanish, "Here, beggar boy, is a centavo for luck."

Cusi could not understand her words, but he understood

her tone of voice and the coin she handed him. Anger froze his blood and pounded in his temples. The centavo rolled across the steps and the beggar crouching there snatched it in haste to hide it away in his filthy rags.

Cusi did not wait to see the Spanish lady helped into her carriage. Blindly he turned and bumped unseeing into a laughing group of *campesino* children. When he tried to push his way clear again, the father laughingly pushed him back into the group. "There you go," he roared playfully in a mixture of Indian and Spanish, "trying to get yourself lost. I'd rather bring all the goats in my flock to market than half this many children." He turned to the woman beside him. "Mamita, help me keep them together." The woman laughed. They were all in holiday mood and willing to be pleased.

The children giggled and whispered, "Papita thinks you are one of us. He never can remember how many we are."

"How many are you?" Cusi asked. He wondered wildly if all this was really happening or if he was having a night-long dream.

The children began counting and naming themselves, everyone talking at once and nobody listening. It sounded to Cusi like, "There's José—Maruka—Francisco—Carlita—Pedro. Francisco is bigger than you, and José is smaller, and Pedro is just the same size." Cusi gave up. He did not know how many children there were or whose names and sizes fitted whom. Suddenly he did not care. He felt in holiday mood too. What did it matter? What did anything matter? He was part of a family!

He was part of a family! He was part of a family! Far away—or did he imagine it—he thought he heard Misti's golden bell, tinkling, tinkling, "Find a family. Find a family."

Cusi was happy. Cusi was bursting with happiness. His golden-sandal bundle rested comfortably against the singing in his heart.

Mamita hurried Papita along. Papita hurried the children. The children pushed each other and laughed and whispered, "What's your name?"

"Cusi," the boy whispered back.

"Oh, that's not a saint's name. That's an Indian name. We will call you Nicho. That one is better." Cusi did not want to have a saint's name. He wanted his Inca name, but no one listened to him.

Papita stopped at a *baile* to look in the windows to see the people dancing. He made Mamita and the children look in the windows to see the people dancing. Cusi thought it was funny and laughed and everyone laughed with him to share his pleasure.

Then Papita spied a Fortune Man with his fortune-telling bird. For a centavo the man would tell the bird to pick out a fortune for the person who had given the money. Papita lined up the children to find enough centavos for each one. Mamita spied Cusi. "That one," she screamed, and tears of laughter streamed down her face, "that one is Indian. He does not belong here."

"No?" Papita was surprised. Then, seeing the hurt in Cusi's eyes, he said quickly, "He belongs here now. I choose him."

All the children danced around Cusi, saying, "This one is Nicho. We choose him to belong to our family." Mamita wiped her eyes and joined the children. "Yes. Nicho is the new one."

Cusi was pleased and yet he was not pleased. He wanted to be a part of a family. He liked this one. They were fun. But he did not feel that he really belonged to them. He felt as if he were playing. Then, too, his name was Cusi. He liked what his name meant. Nicho, to him, was nothing.

Mama and Papa and the children seemed to think all was settled. He was with them. That was enough. Papa had enough centavos and everyone had his little paper-roll fortune that the bird gave them.

Cusi's read, "Grieve not if your searching circles." Mama was comforting. "Many fortunes are like that," she said, "just words, not meaning anything." Cusi said nothing. He had heard these words before. They did mean something. What it was he would know someday. Of that he was certain.

The afternoon slowly turned to evening. Mama and Papa and the children were still having fiesta. Cusi was tired, but he was happy. It was wonderful to know how a family acted when they were together. Gradually he was able to join faces and names together. Francisco was the oldest, a boy about twelve probably. He was very quiet, much more so than his noisy brothers and sisters. He reminded Cusi of Chuto somehow. Quickly the boy put the thought of Chuto from his mind. The lonely old man in the lonely hidden valley had no place here in this fun-loving group.

Mama began hunting a place for them to sleep. They would not be ready to go home to their little ranchito for days and days. In the meantime they would need shelter. Papa hunted for food. He found the market eating place, where stewed meats and coffee and cheese could be bought for a few centavos. He hurried his hungry flock along, loudly proclaiming that it was easier to bring goats and sheep to town than girls and boys.

When time came to pay for the meal there was chattering and searching. Papa had almost enough. Mama had a little more. Finally Francisco found the remaining needed centavos and gave them to the man for the food they had eaten.

Papa laughed. "See," he told Cusi, "it is this way with a family. Those who have anything share it. Those who do not have anything—" Papa laughed and spread his hands out shoulder-high. "If they do not have it, they cannot share. It is nothing." Everyone laughed. They thought Papa had made a wonderful joke. Everyone but Cusi. Cusi felt the golden sandals beneath his poncho and did not laugh because he did not feel that he could ever share them.

After the meal was over Mama found just what she had hoped to find, an empty room belonging to a friend of her aunt's cousin. It was her turn to hurry her tired family to shelter and to sleep. Nicho, the New One, as they called him now, was put to sleep between Francisco and Pedro. Francisco and Pedro slept, but sleep would not come to Cusi. He was not used to closed shelters. His bed had always been under the night sky beside the sleeping Misti.

Somewhere a small bell tinkled and an owl hooted. Somewhere a church bell rang and somewhere people danced to stringed music.

Somewhere an old man sat before a smoldering campfire. Somewhere a proud black llama stayed outside a city gate.

Stealthily Cusi got up. All around him in the room were sleeping people—Mama and Papa, Maruka and Carlita, José and Francisco and Pedro. They were nice people. He liked them. He would remember them always. But he did not belong to them.

He belonged to the Inca. His heart was among the mountain peaks in a hidden valley.

Stealthily he stole out of the room and down the dark

cobblestone streets to the gate in the city wall. The same guardsman was at the gate. "Where do you go, boy?" he challenged.

"To my llamas," Cusi answered.

To his llamas! His heart sang to hear the words. Nearby a llama bell tinkled, "Find a family? Find a family?" A proud black llama stood alone against the night.

Cusi stumbled forward. "Misti!" he called. "Come, llamas. Come, llamas."

"Find a family?" Misti's bell tinkled, and with a soft, glad cry Cusi answered, "Yes, my llamas. Come. We are going home."

16. KEEPER OF THE FIELDS

"Forget us not although we are few in number."

The Sunrise Call rose on the wings of morning, on the wings of sound.

"Forget us not although our Ancient Greatness
is now but a shadow
in the memory of man."

Sweet as a night bird's calling, clear as a day bird's song, the words soared and swelled in the misted morning, blending their rhythm with the rhythm of colors in the sunrise sky.

"Forget us not although our Ancient Pride
is as the dust of the earth
blown before the willful wind."

How good, how right it felt to be again where the Sun in its glory could be greeted with freedom, with voice, with gesture, in the way that was part of the pattern of living.

"Keep our feet straight in thy path,
for we are thy children."

The old Indian finished, his head thrown back, his throat pulsing with the heartbeats of his emotion. Cusi repeated after him:

"For we are thy children,
O Sun. O Sun,
Great Father of the Inca,
We are thy children."

116

Cusi looked around, surprised at the stillness that veiled the meadow he and his llamas had reached after traveling all night long.

Then the old Indian giving the Sunrise Call greeted Cusi. He was a stranger to Cusi. "I saw you coming, you and your llamas. But I could not wait to greet you. The Sun came just then. You and the Sun came into the new day together. It is a good omen."

Cusi laughed. Gone was his shyness of a week ago. He felt happy, so happy that everything else seemed unimportant. Now he said, natural and serious and quietly glad, "I am a good omen. I know it. You see I am going home."

The Indian looked at him for a long time, saying nothing, but the silence was not heavy. It was restful and right, as everything about this new day seemed restful and right. Cusi returned the old man's gaze frankly and with interest. He saw a thin old Indian, bent with the years and the vigor of living. The brown face was wrinkled with age, but the hair above it was black as a young man's, and the black eyes were young and bright and keen. Then Cusi started and looked again. Massive, heavy gold earplugs hung from the man's ears, lengthening the earlobes to fantastic length. The man nodded. "Yes," he said.

Although the answer was short, it carried a wealth of meaning. The man's simple "Yes" told Cusi, "I am one of them, as you are. We belong." A month ago Cusi would have tortured his mind asking himself, "Who are they? To whom do we belong? Why do a few of us wear them?" Now such questions seemed unimportant.

After another time of silence the man spoke. "You have been to Cuzco. Did you bring the golden sandals back with you?"

"Yes." It was Cusi's turn to answer simply. The man seemed satisfied with the answer, as Cusi had been.

Cusi looked around. Misti and the two yellow-brown llamas were standing patiently, their loads gently swaying on their backs. Although they had traveled during the night, they had gone slowly and rested often. They did not seem tired, but Cusi wanted to unload their packs and to feed them. He was standing in a meadow of ychu grass. To one side stretched wide fields of corn and beans. Between the fields and the meadow grass a mountain rivulet tumbled along. Mountain peaks piled high around them. They crowded close in to the meadow and the fields, looking down with friendliness and protection.

As if satisfied with what his searching look had found, the old man said, "Bring them before my hut. I will help you unload them that they may rest and eat."

Misti, understanding the man's tone, or perhaps Cusi's nod of acceptance, turned and led the others across the grass, across the narrow stream to the hut in the field. Cusi and the old man followed. The man was talkative now. "They call me Keeper of the Fields. His Fields. Chuto and I and you too, perhaps, follow the same trail." To Cusi's look of surprise the Indian explained, "I know him as I know you. As I knew you had gone down the mountain trail to Cuzco."

Suddenly Cusi too wanted to talk to this keen, understanding old man. After the llamas had been unloaded and left to feed and to rest in the ychu meadow the young boy sat before the old man and talked to him. White clouds floated against the blue sky, resting their heads on the high peak tops. The little river babbled and sang on its way to join big rivers.

Cusi looked at the bright running water and then he said, "I hope the little river stays here in the lonely mountains, so men won't capture it and hide it under street ways." As if the words had unlocked the door to his heart, Cusi talked on. He told the Old One many things—of his loneliness in Hidden Valley, of his wanting to know the answers to questions that never were answered, of his longing to be part of a family, and finally of the finding of the golden sandals and his journey to Cuzco. "I found a family there," he finished, "or rather they found me, but I felt it was not true. I felt it was make-believe. They were not my family. I could not make them so."

"And the sandals, did you bring them with you?" the Indian asked again.

"Yes, it was the sandals that made me know they could not be my family. I could not share them. If it had been Chuto who needed them, or Misti, I could have given them because— because—" The boy struggled for the right word and suddenly leaped to his feet, his eyes black and deep with his excitement. "They would have had a right to them because we are part of each other. We are a family. We belong to one another and everything we have can be shared together."

Cusi stood still and tense. There was the answer! What he had been looking for had been his. He had not known it. He had almost lost it. He had almost gone away, leaving all that mattered behind him. "But I guess deep in my heart I knew," he said aloud, "because when I traded for one thing at the market, I always traded for two, two knitted caps, two pairs of cotton trousers, two alpaca sweaters. Always one for Chuto, one for me."

The old man was laughing softly. "Of course you knew, but you had to find out that you knew. You will get your heart's desire." He quoted, " 'Grieve not if your searching circles.' "

"Oh!" Cusi cried. "Oh! I understand now. My trail circles back to Hidden Valley. To where I belong."

The Old One pointed skyward. It was midday. Cusi had talked away the hours of morning. "But you did not waste them, Cusi. Their coming was a spring thaw in a mountain river. The ice in your heart has melted. The flood of your feeling has washed clean your life-way of its deadwood of misunderstanding."

Misti's llama bell tinkled impatiently. "It is time that you take the trail again," the old man said kindly. "I will help you load your llamas and find the way."

"I know the trail," Cusi told him. "I traveled it not many days ago."

The Indian shook his head. "That trail is gone. A landslide wiped it away. Almost half a mountain slid down into the valley where the trail forked."

"No! It cannot be. It must not be. That would mean the Allyu town was gone—and the woman who fed me, who called me son—" Cusi stared with unbelieving eyes.

"Perhaps. Year by year our number grows fewer."

"The Inca will never die!" Cusi returned hotly.

"While one of us remains," the other added, and a pool of silence widened as his words dropped heavily into the past that waits to hold words that have been said.

The Indian sighed. "Forget us not," he repeated softly, and it was a farewell for those of his blood who had gone on the trail of no returning. Cusi felt a need for getting home, for being safe again with those he loved and those who loved him, safe again in Hidden Valley. Misti came closer. His sad black eyes were fixed with devotion on his young master's face. He too felt the need of hurry.

"Time passes," the old man said and went first across the field, across the babbling river, across the ychu grass, and in among the dwarfed trees that crowded close together in the folds of the hills at the foot of the mountains. Cusi followed him, and, as was their way, the llamas marched behind in haughty fashion.

When the shadows of evening fell with purple softness over the bleakness of the bare brown mountains, the Keeper of the Fields said good-by to the highland shepherd. "This is for Chuto," he said, handing Cusi an ear of corn. "It is from the Lake," he said, meaning Lake Titicaca, the Sacred Lake of the Ancient Inca. "Chuto will prize it. And this—this is for you. Learn to make it talk, and its voice will heal your heart's loneliness." It was a long reedlike flute that highland people use to sing to themselves and to their flocks. Cusi was pleased. It was the first gift that anyone had given him, and he felt the sting of tears in his eyes. "Today has been the greatest day of your life, for you have learned to read your own heart." With that the old man turned and went back over the trail he had come. He was lost quickly in the purple shadows, and only his memory remained like the small glow of an evening campfire.

Cusi went on. His llamas followed. Somewhere a night bird chirped his evening prayer. Somewhere an old man sat by the blackened chips of a supper fire. Chuto. Waiting.

Night closed in, thick and still, mysterious and cold. Bright stars twinkled down, and a pale moon. On a lonely trail a young boy slept by three tired llamas. In a lonely valley at the glacier edge Suncca, the dog, howled. The llamas did not hum. Even the wind was still.

The Keeper of the Fields walked on slowly. His feet knew this trail. He would not rest until he sat again before the door of his hut, before the fields of beans and corn. He stopped to listen, to peer into the black night shadows. Yes. Someone was coming. He had expected it.

A shadow was beside him, blacker than the night shadows that lurked among the dwarfed trees. The shadow spoke. "Did he come this way?"

"Yes."

"Is he going back to his valley?"

"Yes."

"What did you tell him?"

"Nothing. Chuto is waiting."

"Chuto is waiting; Chuto, who has done his work well. You too, Keeper of the Fields, Keeper of the Inca's children; the seeds you plant grow the food of the Ancients. Our Inca commends you."

The old man bowed his head. "I but keep his fields so that those who pass by need not go hungry on their way. In his name I feed them."

"In his name you keep the links of the chain together." The shadow was gone. The Old One walked alone. He was tired. He was lonely. He was getting old. Who would come to mend the chain when he had gone to be among his Ancients? he wondered. Then he remembered Cusi, and strength returned to him; warmth returned, comforting his heart. "Not yet are we conquered. The Inca shall never die."

Before him lay the meadow of ychu grass and beyond it the little river and then the fields of corn. He, Keeper of the Fields, was home again.

17. WRITTEN IN THE STARS

"Hear the llamas humming, my Misti? They know we are coming home to them." Cusi got out his flute and gave the flute call in answer. He had been practicing it all day as he walked along the trail, and although it was far from perfect it delighted him. Suncca began a wild, excited barking. Chuto appeared at the head of the trail.

Cusi was alarmed at the weariness in the Old One's face, but when Chuto spoke his voice sounded as it always did, soft and patient and kind. "You have come back," the old man said and repeated himself as was his habit. "You have come."

He touched briefly Cusi's shoulder. Together the man and the boy walked to the hut before the supper fire. "Deep in my heart I think I knew you would come back. I think I never doubted it, deep in my heart."

Cusi smiled at him. "Deep in my heart I must have known too, because look, I bartered for these at the market place. One for you. One for me. This for you. This for me." As he talked Cusi unloaded Misti and gave Chuto the things he had brought for him.

Chuto was pleased. He put the trousers on. He put the sweater on. He put the cap on. Then he helped Cusi unload the two other llamas. He never asked where the rest were that had gone down the trail with Cusi. Later on, perhaps, he would ask or Cusi would think to tell him. Right now the important thing was to get the loads off the tired llamas, to turn them into the ychu grass to join the humming herd. Right now the important thing was to get the potatoes and the corn and the coca stored away within the shelter. These things done, the other things would follow, each in its own place and its own way.

While they were eating supper Cusi got out the corn from Sacred Lake, gift to Chuto from the Keeper of the Fields. Chuto's eyes lighted when Cusi gave it to him. "Ah, you saw him, then? You saw him," he said as he thoughtfully turned the corn over and over in his strong brown hands.

"I saw him," Cusi answered. "He showed me the new trail around the landslide. Did you know there was a landslide?"

Chuto nodded. "They told me. How good that you saw her, now that the sliding mountain has, perhaps, destroyed all that you saw." This was what Cusi had wanted—some word, some sign, some token that the Old One wanted to talk.

Cusi moved nearer the small fire flame. The night was hushed with waiting. There were no stars. There was only blackness, velvet blackness, thick and soft, blanketing the mountain peaks, blanketing the wind, hushing the noises of the night.

Cusi spoke. "Chuto, my Chuto, I want to stay here with you. You are my family. This is my home. I never want to go away again."

Chuto did not answer. The llamas were not humming. Even the whining Suncca was still.

"Chuto, let me stay."

"Why do you say that? Why?"

"Because it is what I want. I learned that this is my heart's deep wish."

"Are you certain? Are you sure? Think before you answer. Do not speak quick words that will run away once you have set them free." Chuto's voice was cold and stern.

Cusi shivered, but he did not falter. "I want to stay. I want to share your days and give you mine."

Again Chuto repeated, "Think, Cusi. Be careful of your words."

"I want to stay."

"You are too young to know what you want."

Cusi stood up. "I am old for my years. The minstrel said it. The Amauta said it. The woman who gave me food and called me son thought it; I could tell. The Keeper of the Fields acted toward me as if I were old enough to talk with. I am old for my years. I am old enough to know what I want. You only, question me, doubt me, turn me back when my feet ache to walk the manhood trail."

Cusi's young voice broke. It was not arrogant. It was not proud. It was a wistful, pleading cry. "Chuto, my father. Father of my choice, believe in me."

Chuto too was standing. "Son of my choice, I believe you now. You are ready. It is I who falter because I love you. Give me time to open this door to you that, once opened, closes it-self forever."

Cusi waited. He stood erect and firm. He did not move. Neither excitement nor fear made his heart beat faster or his pulse race. He was relaxed. He was ready. He was not afraid.

At last Chuto spoke. "Four hundred years have lessened our numbers, but have not diluted our blood. For four times four hundred years our blood will flow in its destined channel across our conquered land. Cusi, repeat after me these words I say:

"I, Cusi, Son of the Ancients,
   Son of Nobility,
   Son of Royalty,
   Son of the Last Mighty Inca,
   I, Cusi, shepherd boy of Peru,
      make my sacred, my lasting, my irrevocable vow . . ."

Cusi's voice did not stammer, did not waver as he said:

"I, Cusi, . . .
      make my sacred, my lasting, my irrevocable vow
      for now and for my tomorrows
      until Death takes Life from me."

Chuto asked again, "Are you ready? Are you sure?"

The reply came promptly and clearly. "I am ready. I am sure."

"It is well. Repeat the words I say. Repeat them slowly. Repeat them distinctly. Each word must cut itself into your heart until life's end.

"I vow to keep the secret of the cave.
Now and forever I keep the secret.
Never will I show it except to the Chosen One.
Never will I speak of its hidden bounty
   except to him who will be chosen to follow me.
Never will I speak of this hidden spot.
I will not think of it lest my dreams betray me.
I will not think of it lest my thoughts escape me:
With my blood I will defend my knowledge.
With my blood I make this vow.
With my blood I will keep it."

Cusi repeated the words. He felt a sharp stab of pain, and a drop of blood slowly dripped to the ground beneath his feet.

Again Chuto told him to repeat words that he said to him. This vow was to keep the Inca's llama flock intact, breeding them with wisdom, tending them with knowledge, giving them out with judgment. Again Cusi felt the small sharp stab of pain and knew his life's blood was hostage to his vow.

The third time Chuto recited the vow the boy answered as clearly as he had the first time. This was his promise to serve, to guide, to train, to protect the chosen novice who would be sent to shepherd the flock when Cusi would be taken to rest in the place of his Ancients.

As Cusi repeated the words, "With my blood I make this vow. With my blood I will keep it," the moon thrust the clouds away and lighted the mountain valley in silver gray.

Chuto motioned for the boy to follow him. They went again down the trail to the Sunrise Rock. Chuto touched the stone wall behind the rock. With the flat palms of his hands he touched it. Slowly the massive wall pivoted. Slowly it turned. Slowly it turned, forming an opening to a great cave.

The man and the boy went inside and the rock closed itself behind them. They were in a gigantic rock-hewn room, which was piled from floor to roof with woven bags upon woven bags filled to bursting with powdered gold.

Chuto spoke, but it did not sound like Chuto's voice. The words were precise. They were deadly and cold. Cusi, listening, shivered.

> "They, the Conquerors, came.
> They came swarming into the land
> with hate and with weapons.

They came.
They captured the mighty Inca,
   holding him with chains.
They captured him.
Down the trails of the Andes
   the Indians sent ten thousand llamas,
   carrying bags of gold dust
   to ransom their King.
But they, the Conquerors, killed him.
They killed the Inca,
   fearing his wrath
   if they set him free.
And the ten thousand llamas
   marching down the trails of the Andes
   vanished from the land,
   and with them vanished
   the gold dust, ransom for the King.

Four hundred years men have searched
   to find the llamas
   and to find the gold.
Only two men shall know
   where the llamas are herded.
Only two men shall know
   where the gold is hidden.
Only two men shall know,
   one whose footsteps approach
   the end of the trail,
   one whose young feet stand
   at its beginning.
Only two men shall know.
Only two men shall know.
This has been written in the stars."

The voice stopped. It did not trail away. One second its icy tone filled the room. The next second all sound had stopped and life stood still.

Cusi's wrist hurt, but he was too proud to touch it. He would not even glance at its wound.

Slowly the cave wall opened, although Cusi had seen no move on Chuto's part. Slowly the old Indian and the young one went out into the cold gray of just before the dawn. They did not return up the trail. They sat in the shelter of the rock and listened to the wind wailing the night's departure.

Chuto talked, and Cusi listened. "I myself went for two years. I saw the coastlands and the sea. I saw cities and the people of the cities, but I came back. I took the vow. Then the Old One who trained me died, and Titu was sent to me. But I was too strict. I feared the outside world would get him. It had taken me for two long years. I vowed he would not be tempted as I had been. I was too strict. He ran away. He will never return. I know it now. I should have known it when he sent you, his son, into my keeping.

"I should have known it when he sent your mother's sandals for you to have. If he had come back himself—if I could have talked with him—but he sent the Amauta, his teacher and later your teacher. The Amauta brought you. The Amauta brought the sandals. I know it now. I think I knew it then when he brought you.

"Such a little thing you were, so serious and so quiet—not a noisy, laughing child as Titu was. Your mother—" Chuto stopped. "You saw her before the landslide came." Chuto stopped again, waiting perhaps for questioning. Cusi had no questions, only thoughts.

That was his mother, he thought. She had spoken truly then when she had called him son. That was his mother, and now she was gone. But no. She was not gone. He carried her safely in his memory. He carried her little golden sandals close to his heart; vividly, safely, and forever he would remember.

And Titu, his father, who wanted for his son what he himself could never have. Where was he now? the boy wondered; but he knew that, wherever Titu was, his thoughts were for his son.

Cusi had no questions. He had only thoughts, but his thoughts were good. They left him comfort and peace.

Chuto was talking again. "Herdsmen of the Inca's llamas must be wise and widely traveled. If you like, you are free to go over the trails. Knowing you, I know you will not be tempted to remain as I was tempted. Neither Titu nor I had made our vows before we left. We had nothing to hold to as you have."

"How could I go and leave the llamas?" Cusi asked him.

The old man answered with dignity, "I would be here. There are many years left for me."

"But if something happened to you?" Cusi asked.

"You would be told."

"Yes, I would be told," Cusi said quietly. "Perhaps some day I'll go, but not tomorrow or tomorrow or tomorrow."

The dawn sent forth its herald colors to let men know that day was due. Cusi and Chuto rose to face the east and to salute the Sun for a new beginning.